Jahanara

Sukumaran is a Tamil poet, writer, translator and editor. He has published nine volumes of poems, two novels, six collections of articles on art, literature and social issues, and compiled and edited four volumes of modern writing by pioneers T. Janakiraman, Mauni, A. Madhavan and Jayakanthan. He has translated from Malayalam into Tamil works by Vaikkom Mohammed Basheer, K. Satchidanandan, Paul Zacharia, Adoor Gopalakrishnan and Unni R., and translated into Tamil through English poems by Pablo Neruda, novels by Gabriel Garcia Marquez, Allasandro Barricco, Ayfer Tunc, and historical writing by Rysard Kapuscinski. His poems have been translated into Malayalam, Hindi, Bengali, Gujarati, Marathi, Punjabi, English, German and French. He served as the editor of the Tamil magazine *Kungumam* and the chief news editor at *Surya*, a Malayalam television channel. He is now the executive editor of *Kalachuvadu*, a Tamil alternative magazine for art and ideas. He was awarded the IYAL Award by the Tamil Literary Garden, Canada in 2017 and the Codissia Lifetime Achievement Award in 2023.

Kalaivani Karunakaran is a freelance editor, translator and independent researcher. She translates between Tamil and English. Her doctorate was in literary spatial studies from the Department of English, University of Madras. Her areas of interest include Sangam Literature, Australian Aboriginal Literature and Translation Studies. She is also a vainika (Carnatic vocalist) and a Kalaripayattu practitioner. She currently teaches in the post graduate department of English, SDNB Vaishnav College, Chennai.

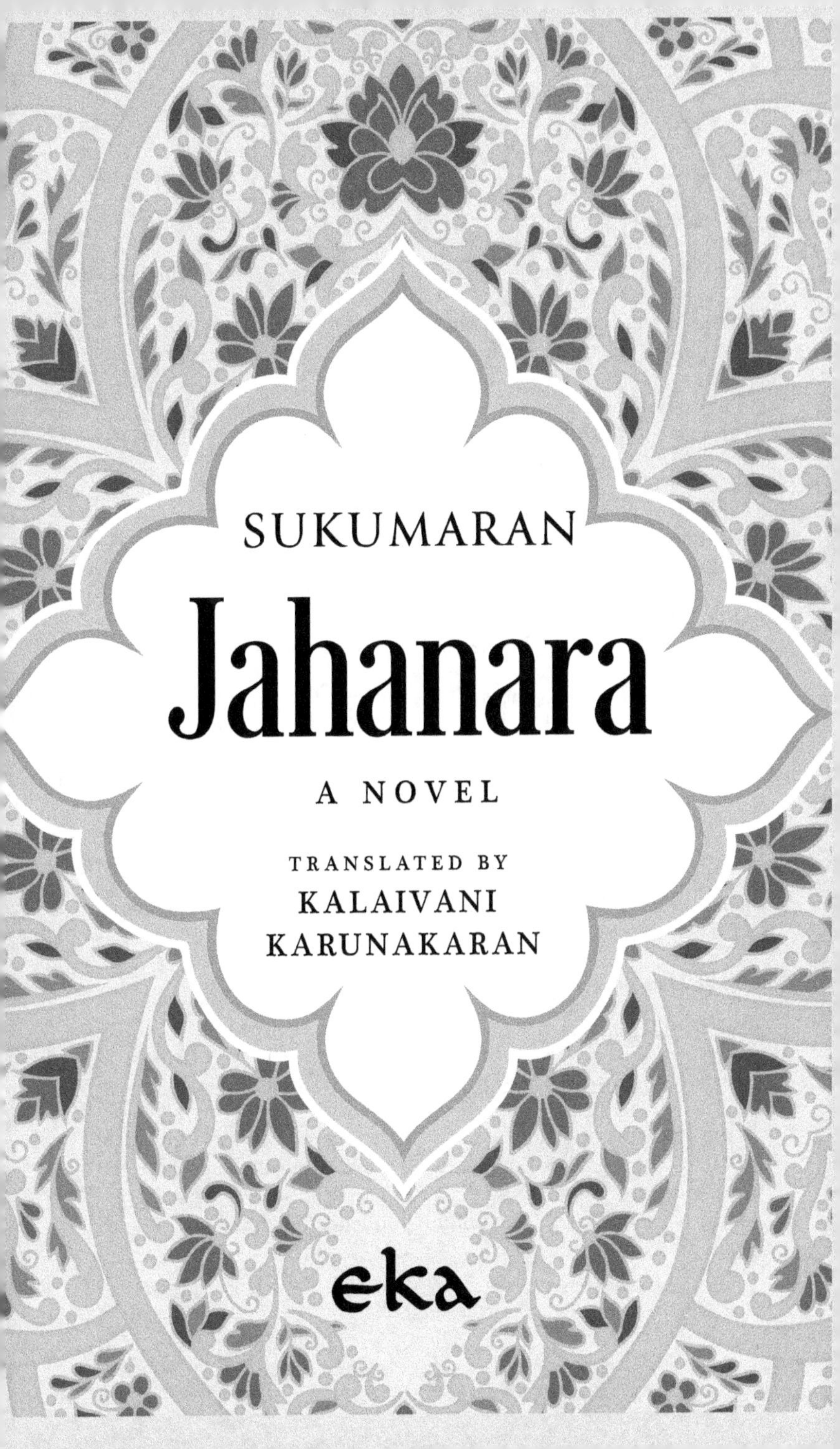

SUKUMARAN

Jahanara

A NOVEL

TRANSLATED BY
KALAIVANI
KARUNAKARAN

eka

eka

First published in Tamil as *Peruvali* in 2017 by Kalachuvadu Publications

Published in English as *Jahanara* in 2024 by Eka, an imprint of Westland Books, a division of Nasadiya Technologies Private Limited

No. 269/2B, First Floor, 'Irai Arul', Vimalraj Street, Nethaji Nagar, Alapakkam Main Road, Maduravoyal, Chennai 600095

ISBN: 9789360457686

10 9 8 7 6 5 4 3 2 1

Typeset by Jojy Philip, New Delhi

Printed at Manipal Technologies Limited, Manipal

TRANSLATING JAHANARA

Jahanara Begum (1614–1681) was the most powerful of Mughal princesses, about whom precious little is known. Sukumaran's *Peruvali* takes one through the gallery of Jahanara's life. It's a work in which history is tightly interwoven with fiction. She comes alive as a powerful princess, a loving daughter, a brilliant diplomat, a young girl caught in the painful crosscurrents of love, and finally, a woman whose freedom and desires were tossed into men's battle for power. As the 'veil' of gender and Mughal tradition weighs heavily on her, she is left with no space to express herself, to sing the sorrows of her muffled heart. However, she did create her own space in writing, which is evident in her epitaph. This poses the first challenge to the translator.

Jahanara must have used Urdu, apart from the several other languages she knew. Her secret diaries were written in Persian, and they were later translated into English. The available sources on Jahanara are in English. So, the Jahanara of *Peruvali* herself is a translation in a way. This translation oscillates between cultures and between history and fiction. Through these oscillations, Jahanara and her veiled words come alive in Tamil. My challenge was to retain both—the prevalent Mughal flavour in the Tamil original, and the linguistic medium used to contain the flavour, its own cultural overtones. Apart from these, retaining the poetic sensibility that pervades the source text was another challenge.

The touch of Mughal sensibilities and the Tamil language work as warp and weft in weaving the majestic picture of Jahanara in this novel. However, achieving a similar frame in English was more challenging.

Apart from the inclusion of Urdu terms and references to Islamic rituals and conventions, evoking a sense of space also played a significant role in recreating the Mughal ethos in the translated text. The descriptions of the Agra, Delhi and Deccan territorries worked in different ways. To begin with, they lent a poetic touch; secondly, they helped establish a perfect backdrop; and finally, they also functioned as metaphors for the changing seasons in human lives. It was challenging to retain all these strands in the translation.

These challenges were the oxymora of pleasure and pain, just like Jahanara's love. Overcoming these challenges left me with a sigh of relief, if not the joy of victory. This relief wouldn't have been possible without other hands or rather heads and hearts at work along me. Many friends broke their heads alongside me over the right choice of words and the fine-tuning of sentences. They are people who made sure I never struggled alone.

I want to thank Geetha Sukumaran, my mentor (and saviour on several occasions), for introducing me to Jahanara. Without her, this work wouldn't have been possible. I also want to thank Latha ma'am, the head of the English Department, Stella Maris College, who introduced me to Geetha akka. I want to convey my sincere thanks to the author of this novel, Sukumaran, for his patience, his trust and for helping with the words and terms I found challenging. I'm grateful for a sentence he said over a call: 'I know my translator.' It made me happy, it made me feel more responsible but also nervous.

I sincerely thank Dr D. Venkataramanan, my research supervisor, for his support throughout the process of translation. His 'supervisorly' approach—fixing deadlines for the submission of the chapters, discussions, suggestions and corrections—took me back to my research scholar days and the thrill of thesis submission. I also thank 'Rawm', who frequently came to my rescue. His microscopic eyes always gave valid suggestions and his Google-like mind always gave the most amazing expressions or equivalents every time I felt helpless while caught in a maze of words.

Kalaivani Karunakaran

He is the one who lives
He is immortal.
Let nothing
but green grass shroud my tomb ...
This is enough to cover this poor one's tomb.
Fakira Jahanara, the annihilated,
The disciple of wise ones,
daughter of Emperor Shah Jahan
May the Almighty Manifest His proofs

—The inscription on Jahanara Begum's tomb
at the Nizamuddin Dargah, Delhi

PART I

CHAPTER I

PANIPAT

My name is Panipat. Whether Panipat was my hometown or I was born there, I do not know. I do not even know when I was born or to whom. What I do know is that I was sold in the slave market, bought by someone from the palace and raised as one among hundreds of eunuchs. Later on, I was appointed to the service of the palace, where I bore witness to the rise and fall of three great emperors. Now, I am the head of the eunuchs in the palace.

For the palace-dwellers and the retinue—in the eyes of men—I am unwanted flesh, a hijra, a eunuch—both an auspicious and inauspicious creature. For the women in the zenana, I am nature's betrayal, a drop that should have coagulated into a female but which, instead, fell down as a male from the climactic peak of creation. This is the reason behind their pity and concern for me.

But I am neither. I don't have any gender. Do I possess the femininity of a male body or the masculinity of a female body? I don't know. Just as Time has passed through me, I have passed through Time—from Emperor Akbar's reign till Shah Jahan's. May Allah forgive me for this vanity but I am above and beyond Time. I am an unsolvable puzzle—just like God. However, people count me as a male. Don't they worship Allah the Supreme Being with immeasurable grace as a male? Is that why Jahanara addresses me as a male? When others treat me like an inanimate object, worse than they would treat their pets, it is she who treats me like a human being. She is my Begum Sahiba—the most glorious of all princesses.

It is still fresh in my memory—the moment in which I greeted her as 'Begum Sahiba' and the radiance the words called forth on her face.

They were locked inside destiny's prison then: the present emperor was Prince Khurram, who was yet to become Emperor Shah Jahan. Empress Mumtaz Mahal was just Arjumand Banu Begum. They, who should have been emperor and empress were trapped in destiny's prison—the Nizam Shahi of the Deccan territory. Destiny had a name: Noor Mahal—the light of the palace. Emperor Jahangir's wife and Shah Jahan's stepmother. What an irony! To call the darkness of the palace by that name—to call a new moon the full moon. Jahanara never referred to the empress using that name. 'Serpent!' she would say, disgustedly. She would pounce on me whenever I hesitantly said, 'She can be cruel. But she is your grandmother. Your Abba's mother. You shouldn't call her that.'

'My grandmother? She's just a stepmother to Abba— that's all. To me, she is a venomous serpent. I hate her.

Not just I, but the whole world hates her. But no one dares to express their hatred, for everyone is afraid of her, of her powers. She could be Noor Mahal the Empress to them, but to me, she is a venomous serpent that coils around me every night, stings and pours venom into my thoughts and dreams.'

When she said this, Jahanara's face would turn red as blood. Her eyes would widen. Her plump cheeks would stiffen. In fact, it was *her* face that resembled the hood of an enraged serpent, then.

I knew the reason for Jahanara's fury. Three years ago, Empress Noor Mahal had taken her elder brother Dara and her younger brother Aurangzeb to Delhi as hostages. They were children then: Dara was ten and Aurangzeb was seven. It was Noor Mahal's decree in Jahangir's name. She had accused her stepson Prince Khurram of plotting a revolt against the emperor, spreading the rumour throughout the empire. But everyone knew that it was not the truth. Even the emperor himself knew it. However, he could not openly defy the empress. Perhaps he was unable to even make sense of it. None but Noor Mahal had access to his mind. She pushed him to such a state, adding a cruelly excessive amount of opium to his drinks, ignoring the warnings of the royal physicians. Emperor Jahangir blindly trusted his wife. She had successfully muddied his mind with her baseless hatred for Shah Jahan. So Emperor Jahangir too began to hate Shah Jahan without any reason. He sent military forces to capture his unruly son and teach him a lesson. Two conditions were put forth for Shah Jahan to be forgiven for his treason against the empire and the emperor. The first condition was that the Deccan territory, under Prince Khurram at the time, be immediately handed over to the emperor's royal secretary; and the second condition was that Khurram's two sons be sent to the Delhi durbar as hostages. The second condition seemed harmless. It was good for the grandchildren to grow up under their grandfather's care—away from the merciless heat of the Deccan plateau. However, Khurram was able to see through the first condition—Noor Mahal's covert tricks, her conspiracy to usurp his right to the throne after Jahangir, would insidiously pave a path to the throne for his half-brother Shahryar, Noor Mahal's own son, who was the emperor's royal secretary at the time. Khurram had no choice but to give in. And so he did.

I wasn't sure whether it was one of Noor Mahal's tricks or the emperor's grace, but Prince Khurram and his family were permitted to stay in Nizam Shahi. However, entry to the royal palace was denied to them. Huge tents were put up. One of them was Khurram's durbar. Four more tents: one each for his wives; one for the servants and maids; and four or five for the royal secretaries and bodyguards. All the tents were spacious. The smallest ones had enough space to accommodate two elephants. A palace could have been built with the money that was spent on these tents, but the possibility of delay justified the building of tents.

The tents had everything—curtains made with gold thread, food served on plates of gold, drinks served in emerald-studded goblets. Prince Khurram was there, and so was Arjumand Banu Begum. Fourteen-year-old Jahanara, twelve-year-old Shuja and three-year-old Murad were also there. There were thirty servants exclusively at Jahanara's service. Of course, it wasn't the palace, but it had all the luxuries of a palace. Jahanara would say only one thing was missing. I would ask, 'What is it?' knowing very well what it was. Within a moment, tears welling up in her eyes and her voice choking, she would say, 'Freedom.'

Only Jahanara could utter that word. Only she could feel it. Even amidst all the luxuries and merriments, I had seen the fire in her eyes. For the other women in the harem, the word freedom had no meaning at all. They were slaves to luxury, which got them whatever they wanted. Though Jahanara also loved comfort and luxury, she had a lust for power. Just fourteen at the time, she was wise enough to give political advice to her father. With a mastery over Persian, she was also a scholar of the Hindu puranas. Her Quran recitals were divine, and she could debate with mullahs and historians. And, yet, despite these accomplishments, she had a rankling, unquenchable thirst for freedom—a thirst restlessly flapping its wings to soar above the earth. The incarceration in the tents, behind muslin curtains, drove her to desperation.

'I don't even have the liberty to sleep peacefully, or even dream, Panipat. When I close my eyes, that serpent, that old hag haunts me.'

I assumed that she had imagined Noor Mahal as a serpent, having heard stories about her in the zenana.

She refused. 'No. It's not my imagination. Wasn't she protected by a serpent?' The fierceness of Jahanara's refusal made me suspect that the story could be true.

Noor Mahal was a Parsi's daughter. Her parents, a bankrupt couple, came to Hindustan in search of a livelihood. Her mother was in the last month of pregnancy. Their journey from Persia had been a gruelling one; they had passed through rough paths, braving the burning sun and freezing cold. And they had finally arrived in an unknown land with an unknown language. An alien land without a single soul to give them water or food. It was difficult for them to survive. How could they, under such circumstances, nurture one more soul? Leaving the infant in the place where it was born, they moved on, believing that some merciful traveller would save the baby. However, guilt began to haunt and torture their souls, and they came back to the place where they had left the infant. Stones had melted under the scorching sun and the place was brimming with the waves of a mirage. A desolate spot without even the shade of a blade of grass. They suspected that the infant, moist with the womb's fluid, would have died in the heat. But when they reached the spot, the sound of the infant dispelled their doubts, and they shuddered at the sight before them: their baby was squirming under the shade of a huge snake's hood.

'Didn't this *iblis* grow up feeding on the serpent's poison? She escaped the poisons of many. Isn't that because her blood has the deadliest venom of all? It is this venom that the old hag spews in my dreams. That is why I cannot sleep.'

I could not agree with Jahanara. Nor could I disagree. My age and experience hesitated to believe the words of a fourteen-year-old girl. But her contracted, reddened eyes spoke for her white nights. Sati-al-Nisa, the personal maid of Arjumand Banu Begum and Jahanara's teacher, pointed out that she was inattentive. Jahanara's stepmother Indira gossiped in the zenana that the young girl had lost her mind, but that was because Khurram paid no heed to her these days, neither did he visit her chamber. Indira sought her revenge through Jahanara. I understood this, but I couldn't tell anyone. Eunuchs never disclose secrets.

Jahanara's grief affected me as well. She was but a newly blossomed flower. I prayed for her: 'Ya Allah, grant peace of mind to this young girl.' I went to her tent, at an hour when she preferred staying alone. The heat of the Deccan air was less harsh that day. I sat in the reading hall, a few steps away from her curtained chamber where she had been lying, and I read to her from *Baburnama*. I was reading the part where her great grandfather spoke about control over one's mind. That was when I addressed her for the first time as Begum Sahiba.

'You are not here, Begum Sahiba.'

Hearing this, she sat up, facing me. Her tears glistened under the light of the hanging lamps. The muslin curtains around her chamber couldn't hide them. This must have come as a surprise to her: a prisoner in a tent being addressed as the princess of all princesses. Her father had not ascended the throne, he hadn't been anointed yet. So what? She was still my Begum Sahiba.

I drew apart the curtains and placed my palm on hers. I could feel the warmth of her soft, shivering hands.

'Begum Sahiba, please tell your Ammi about your nightmares. She will consult astrologers. Your nightmares may hold the key to open our prison.'

The next day, Arjumand Banu Begum met her daughter in Kushal Khana. Prince Khurram and the astrologer Abul Faizi heard their conversation from the other side of the curtains. I also heard them from a short distance. The astrologer examined the princess's charts and explained the positions of the planets. In the next few weeks, Scorpio would be at its peak; the bad dreams were a result of that. But they wouldn't harm the princess. He also suggested remedies. Sighs of relief shook the tents, and the radiance of a full moon returned to Jahanara's face.

After the others had left, Begum Sahiba came to me. She had a string of pearls in her hands that glittered in the chandelier's light. She put it in my hands and said, 'My reward to you. For finding the keys to unlock our prisons.'

I touched the reward. Large pearls strung in a gold chain! Of course, I like jewels. I am also a woman after all—I like bangles, rings and *passa*. But I am more interested in uncut jewels. Is that because I am an unfulfilled creature?

Looking at the smile on Jahanara's face, I said, 'Thank you, Begum Sahiba.'

CHAPTER 2

Jahanara saw two contradictory visions in the same dream. She was present in both.

The durbar is on. The Diwan-e-Aam. The emperor and ministers are present. It is not clear whether the one on the throne is Abba. She stands behind the *jharokha* as usual.

Her body rises and hovers above the ground; her garments loosen and transform into clouds; her pearl necklaces, bangles and bracelets come off and turn into shafts of light. Her shawl, woven with golden threads and pearls, twirls, twists and becomes rope-like—and then it squirms and transforms into a fork-tongued serpent emitting fire. Jahanara's body is set ablaze. Clouds and stars rise, touching her body. The blueness diminishes into darkness.

Unable to bear the heat, her scorched body begins to drop to the ground, turning into a ball of fire. As it is falling, a pair of large lotus-like hands catch her. Touched by their coolness, the fire is put out ...

Jahanara jumped off her bed, drenched in sweat. The air that entered the tent scorched her like a lick of fire.

She drank some water from a pot. She poured the rest of it on her right palm and dabbed it on her face. 'Ya Allah, what kind of a dream is this? Is it for good or bad? I don't know. Whom can I ask for an explanation at this hour of the night?'

She lifted the curtains at the tent's entrance and looked outside. There was no light in most of the tents. There was movement of dim shadows in a few. The lights were still on in the servants' tents. So some people were awake. Their conversations in hushed tones were audible. She could ask Ammi. She had enough experience in such things. Squinting her eyes, she looked in the direction of Arjumand Bano's tent. The curtains at the sides were drawn yet the silhouette was visible. Columns of light escaped from inside the tent through the holes at the top. Ammi was still awake. That meant Abba was with her. Abba could not stay without Ammi, even in the battlefield. He had three wives apart from Ammi. But he saw something in Ammi that he did not in the others. When Jahanara thought what it could be, she felt a flutter in her navel.

She felt a tickling sensation between her ribs, as if two lillies had blossomed. She tried to shake off the untoward thought. Just then, she heard the call of again: 'Devi ....' She felt wet lips pressed on her forehead. She touched her forehead. It was moist but not from her sweat.

Why do such dreams haunt me? A few days ago, that serpent Noor Mahal ruined my sleep. When I got rid of her, this dream arrived. Earlier, my dreams were terrifying, whereas this is exciting but unsettles the soul. Who called me 'Devi' so longingly, just like Nala called Damayanti. Whose hands were they which held me when I slipped?

Jahanara felt as if she were descending into unending spirals of bushes. A cold breeze chased away the stifling heat of the Deccan. She returned to bed. She lay down and covered herself from top to toe with a sheet, gripping its edges tightly, so that the wet lips and lotus-like hands wouldn't come near her again. She heard the footsteps of the guard on night watch. She counted them. Before they faded away, she was descending a stairway that wouldn't end.

'Begum Sahiba, don't get upset so by these dreams. This is just a trick that your age plays. Every young woman has such dreams at your age. That's what the physicians in the durbar say. Such dreams are common when the female body and mind are blossoming. They are a sign that a girl is ready to enter into womanhood. These dreams foretell that someone is going to come for you. Which Prithviraj is going to come on a horse to take away this Samyukta?' Panipat said.

'Don't give false reasons to comfort me, Panipat. Both of us know very well that none of these things will ever happen. What I read in Emperor Akbar's book was news to me. But you were present in court when it was declared, weren't you? Then why do you sprinkle empty words over me?'

Panipat bowed his head. His plump hands were stroking his grey, smoke-like beard. His large body, brimming with femininity, was swaying to the tunes of his thoughts.

Emperor Akbar had declared that princesses from his royal lineage would not be allowed to marry. Because this may lead to conflicts between the male heirs and the offsprings born through marriages outside of the royal family. Such conflicts and possible revolts could put the empire at risk. This was the result of his fear that his dream for a peaceful nation may perish. None of the later heirs were exempted from this rule. But rivalries often sparked and exploded within the family. The princesses felt stifled, caught between their sighs of yearning. They found some solace in one another, behind the curtains of the zenana. Unable to voice their desires, they spoke with their eyes. The hundreds of wives and concubines of the empire offered their own selves to quench the carnal hunger of princesses. A few quenched their thirst secretly.

Different kinds of people came to Emperor Jahangir's durbar at Diwan-e-Aam: princes, minor kings, merchants, scholars, heads of mutts, imams, mullahs, Sufi fakirs, priests, Englishmen, Parsis, Turks and Afghans. Such visits would unsettle the zenana. The secret whispers and hushed laughter with the visitors would rouse the harem. The women would rush to get a spot in the balcony when the durbar was on. They peered through the gaps in the jharokha to catch a glimpse of the new guests. Mehrunnisa—one of the concubines of the emperor—also longed to see someone.

A British man from the East India Company came to the durbar. His eyes reflected the stars that shone behind the curtains—the diamonds set in the jewels of the ladies in attendance. He was enamoured of two jewels in particular—alive and blinking—Mehrunnisa's eyes. He visited every day while the durbar was in session—just to look at those eyes. Even while conversing with the emperor, his eyes would be searching for Mehrunissa. On a blessed day, a strong wind ruffled and lifted the curtains. The British gentleman's eyes forgot to blink. Mehrunnisa's, too, did not falter.

Soon they were crazy about each other. With the help of one of the eunuchs in the harem, they met in secret. But somehow, this reached the cruel ears of Noor Mahal. The British gentleman was immediately summoned to the court, and the emperor commanded him to leave for Britain immediately. After that, no one saw Mehrunnisa in the zenana. No one, except Noor Mahal, knew what happened to her. No one was able to find out who had helped arrange the secret meetings between Mehrunnisa and her British lover. No hijra ever reveals their secrets.

Panipat stopped stroking his beard and looked up at Jahanara.

'Begum Sahiba, I am not intelligent enough to divine the meaning of your dreams, but I can assure you that nothing unfortunate will befall you. What I said was not a lie. A man will come for you. You will be his heart and soul. He will never go against your will. Just wait and watch. Begum Sahiba, of all the women I have seen in the zenana, you are the bravest. This is not flattery. You cannot be the empress, of course. It is not your misfortune but Hindustan's. But you will rule. Do not ask this slave how. I do not know that.'

Jahanara looked into Panipat's eyes for a moment. Then she smiled. It turned into a laugh, and then exploded into a guffaw. She laughed till her eyes watered and her words slurred. She shook, covering her face with a towel. After a long laugh, she wiped her face with the towel.

'Panipat, no one has made me laugh so much in my lifetime, especially during this imprisonment. A *sabbaash* for that. Isn't it a great lie? To tell someone like me who gets terrified by a mere dream that I am brave and that I will rule? Isn't it delusional to call a coward a braveheart?'

A calm Panipat said, 'Begum Sahiba, say what you want, but what I said is bound to happen. May the benevolent Allah keep me alive till then. Whatever I said is true. Why should you doubt your bravery? Bravery is not courage alone but a combination of daring, ingenuity and fear. There is no bravery without fear.'

Jahanara thought, What this innocent Panipat says is true. I have all the traits he describes. I can talk to Abba about the rule. I can roam around not caring a jot about Noor Mahal. But I can also be afraid of dreams. Is this fear of dreams a result of this bravery? Are the dreams an outcome of the fear that I may never get to experience the male touch? If that's fear, then what is the meaning of the hands that held me so lovingly?

Panipat knew the answer, but he did not want to say it. He remained silent. Jahanara looked at him as if he might give the answer. A bodyguard's voice was heard just then, tearing through the silence.

'A'la Azad Abul Muzaffar Shahab-ud-Din Mohammad Khurram is dead!'

Jahanara was stunned. Arjumand Banu Begum's scream rang out from her tent and shook the entire place.

CHAPTER 3

PANIPAT

I was unable to be by Khurram's side when he breathed his last, and this plunged me into grief. Guilt weighed heavier than the bereavement. I was the first to see him set foot in this world from Taj Bibi's womb; the first to touch his soft body, to hear his first cry, to respond to his first call and to take him in my arms. All this was Allah's grace. I was a witness to his life—as an infant, a child, a young man and a thirty-five-year-old brave man, asserting his right to the throne. I was with him throughout, except in his final moments. It is this slave's misfortune.

Several months after our move to the Deccan, someone spread the rumour that Khurram had put together an army against Emperor Jahangir. The emperor bought into the rumours, intoxicated as he continually was with liquor and heroin. Just a nod from Noor Mahal was enough to convince him. As a punishment for this, Khurram and his retinue were driven away to Nizam Shahi and imprisoned within the tents. An important truth had eluded the emperor's memory: it was Khurram who had brought the Deccan territory under Mughal rule.

Parsis were a threat to Jahangir's rule. Gandhara, under Persian rule, too feared the Mughals. This mutual fear led to conflicts between the two. Shahryar led the regiment for the last conflicts. Khurram refused to go along or send his army. This fuelled the rage of Emperor Jahangir and Noor Mahal. It was true that Khurram had complaints against the emperor's rule and he expressed his displeasure through his words. However, this charge against him was baseless. It was clear as daylight that Khurram would inherit the throne. Would anyone aim an arrow at the fruit just a few yards away from one's hand? That too someone as intelligent as Khurram? I couldn't believe this.

One of the servants in the prince's tent described Khurram's last moments. His narration seemed genuine, but I was not able to believe it. I sensed a mysterious gap lurking between truth and falsity.

On a mat, sprawled on the floor lay Khurram, shrunken and grey. One of his ministers was telling Arjumand Banu Begum that the royal physicians were on their way. In front of them was a brass vessel with the prince's blood, phlegm and urine—for the physicians to examine. The burning agarwood dispelled the stink with its smoke. Khurram tried to get up and say something. It wasn't words but his blood that gushed out of his mouth. It flowed over his chest and splashed on his sides. His head drooped. Two servants held his weak body. He let out a cry, which sounded like the squawk of an arrow-stricken peacock, and fell down on the mat. The physician came running and checked his pulse. He looked up at the minister and the begum and shook his head. Begum fell on Khurram's lifeless body. Her cries ripped through the tents.

Lamps were lit again, and the sleepy tents woke up one by one. Jahanara shot out of her tent. I struggled to keep pace with her. The women in the harem and the hijras rushed past us. But everyone except me and Jahanara was stopped at the entrance to the prince's tent. The minister stopped the other three wives of Khurram too and explained the situation. Enraged and tensed, they got into an argument with him.

Arjumand Banu Begum was lying on the ground, hugging Khurram. She looked lifeless herself for a moment. Jahanara cried 'Abba' and collapsed next to the begum. I noticed blood stains on Begum's face and upper garment.

Khurram's absence plunged everyone into an abyss of sorrow. Everyone except for two, who felt differently. His death brought relief to the Rajput prince who was the ruler of the Deccan territory. Khurram was the heir to the throne, he would be emperor one day, which unnerved the Rajpur prince. He had been reduced to a ruler in name only on his own soil under Khurram's rule. He had to be careful and humble before Noor Mahal as she was the emperor's wife. But now there was no need. I saw his face beaming with the joy of freedom. He hastened the arrangements to take Khurram's body to Agra.

With all her plans thwarted, Noor Mahal's face had turned ashen. She had strongly wished Khurram would never return to Delhi. That was why she had driven him away to the Deccan. As per the emperor's commands, he was sent to the Deccan to oversee the administration. Khurram knew what it meant—an indirect imprisonment. He obeyed the orders, but his thoughts constantly pursued the paths to Agra, especially for the sake of Jahanara and Arjumand Banu Begum. This was what I too was ardently praying for. Of course, I was selfish. I was used to living in the havens of the palace; I was used to the *attar*-inebriated wind around it and the coolness of the greenery there—I could not bear the heat wave in the Deccan. But I never imagined Khurram would find a way out of here.

The howdah and elephant were ready. Bathed and laid in a sandalwood casket, Khurram's body was also ready to be taken to Agra. Arjumand Banu allowed no one near the coffin, except the chief minister and me. Neither did she leave the place for a moment. Khurram's other wives were forbidden inside the howdah and were enraged, but they were too helpless to voice their anger.

The journey began before the first rays of sunlight tore open the skies. There were very few in the retinue: the chief minister; Arjumand Bano Begum; Jahanara and her sister Roshanara and her brothers Shuja and Murad; the royal astrologer Abul Faizi; pantrymen; Karim Chand; Khan Jahan Lodi, Khurram's most trustworthy commander-in-chief; and I. There were a few soldiers and hijras to help, and a few cooks too. We had to leave behind several cooks because a few hijras were known for their excellent culinary skills. The ponies carried all our food. This retinue was not even one-fourth of what had reached Nizam Shahi from Agra. The remaining crowd was decreed to stay back at Nizam Shahi till further orders. Our retinue moved on, leaving behind shock and lamentation.

This must have been the smallest retinue in the entire Mughal dynasty. Whether it was to attend the *Duhur* prayers on Fridays or while touring the kingdom, it would seem as if an entire city followed the royal family. What followed Khurram's coffin was not even a street's crowd.

It wasn't a slow journey, but it took us twenty days to cross the deserts of the Deccan. The winter scorched the days and froze the nights. It almost felt like a rebirth when we reached Fatehpur Sikri.

Arjumand Banu Begum and the chief minister announced that we would enter Agra only on an auspicious day.

'What foolishness is this, Panipat? What difference would an auspicious or inauspicious day make to those who have lost everything? We have returned with Abba's lifeless body'—came a hushed reprimand from Jahanara.

'Begum Sahiba, what can I say? I am but a poor slave, I have no say in the decisions of the chief minister and the begum.'

Jahanara did not reply. Instead, she turned inwards, delving deeper and deeper into her thoughts. Her withered face reflected the fatigue from the long journey home and despair at her father's death. Her movements betrayed her state of mind—she seemed afraid and unhinged. She was Khurram's only child who was born during peaceful times, the only child who wasn't born when he was at war. When she was born, I heard Arjumand Banu Begum telling Khurram, 'She is the only one who will give you a sense of peace.' Khurram trusted his begum's words. Jahanara was with him on all his journeys. Despite the age difference, he discussed everything with her. Jahanara's suggestions were never rejected outright by her father Khurram, who was the son of Emperor Jahangir and the heir to the Mughal throne. He admired her intelligence and adored her beauty. No wonder all his other children, except Dara, envied Jahanara. I was never able to imagine a horizon for the love they had for each other.

This eternal love prompted the question: 'When Abba himself is no more, what is the meaning of these rituals?'

I said, 'Begum Sahiba, I have no idea why we are prolonging this,' but I knew that Asaf Khan had come to meet us.

'Is Nana coming?' Her face blossomed like a dew-drenched rose from the relief at receiving a helping hand. Asaf Khan was her maternal grandfather, Arjumand Banu Begum's father, and Noor Mahal's brother. But he and Noor Mahal were as different from each other as an eagle and a dove.

The coffin was kept in the palace of Fatehpur Sikri, at the centre of the durbar hall. Asaf Khan arrived with his retinue. Those who had left Nizam Shahi after us had also arrived by now. Our delay had given them enough time to catch up and reach Agra. Khurram's wives and others were also there. The smell and smoke of agarwood, attar and frankincense choked the hall. A similar layer of smoke, without any smell, had blurred Asaf Khan's eyes. He wiped his face with both his hands and rubbed his eyes in an effort to fight back his tears. He gestured to start the necessary rituals. Jahanara began to sob. Arjumand Banu Begum remained composed, and this roused my laughter. Could I laugh? No. I stiffened my face. The impending climax of a well-known play tickled my senses and I wasn't able to hide it. My hands shivered. This attracted Jahanara's attention. She raised her eyebrows in suspicion. Before I could open my mouth to give a clarification, the coffin's lid was lifted up. Khurram, whose slender body lay still in the coffin until then, sprung out of it, smiling, and mocking Time—like a sunrise on the horizon. Asaf Khan was stunned. His wives let out cries of surprise and excitement from behind the curtains. Arjumand Banu Begum stood rooted to the spot. Jahanara was about to fall down, when I moved quickly to prop her up. I whispered in her ears, 'Begum Sahiba, this was what I meant by instinct. This is the statecraft and bravery I was telling you about.'

For more than three generations, I have been witnessing the means and tactics human beings use to attain power: humiliation, gift of the gab, showers of love, relationships, rejection of relationships, backstabbing, celebration of victories, forgetting everything after victory and ruling over everyone. Those in power dream of eternal rule. They remain buried within their dreams.

What had just been staged was one such powerplay. I had borne witness to the dreams of so many rulers—from Akbar to Jahangir. And how many more dramas were yet to be witnessed? What had just happened right in front of my eyes was one such circus for power. I too had played a small part in it. I burst into laughter when I thought about it. It got lost amidst the roar of laughter celebrating the reincarnation of Khurram.

'What's this, Panipat? You knew about this charade and feigned ignorance all this while. Tell me what really happened!'

'What do I know, Begum Sahiba? What do you want me to say? I was with you throughout, like your own shadow. Where did I ever go without you? When have I ever left you?' I tried to wriggle out of the fix but could not. Would my tricks work on the counsellor to the future emperor?

'You were there with me in Abba's tent that night, but then you disappeared later. Not just you but Ammi too, the chief minister and Sati as well. Everything makes sense now: all of you had vanished behind a "screen" for your "rehearsal". Tell me now, Panipat— what happened? What actually transpired that night?'

At first, Jahanara's pleas seemed like that of a little girl's. Finally, it turned into a royal princess's order. Or did I imagine that? When I was thinking about this, she interrupted again, 'Tell me now! Why do you hesitate?'

Yes, an order it was. Hearing this, the flame of the wall lamp stilled for a moment and then flickered. Can anyone go against a princess's order?

CHAPTER 4

That night Panipat pleaded with Jahanara in the study hall: 'Begum Sahiba, it's the duty of us eunuchs never to reveal the secrets we know, at any cost. Even if cut down with swords or burnt alive. The walls of this harem and the feet of our elephants know the fate of those who reveal secrets. Do you want me to give up this duty for your sake? Aren't you plunging me into deep trouble?'

After a long time, he was enjoying reading *Akbarnama* in a spacious chamber of the Fatehpur Sikri palace under the canopy of a generous light. He read in the tent's shade too at Nizam Shahi. But that wasn't soothing to the heart. It was like holding a lamp against a strong wind. Here, it was like flying on one's own. His reading got interrupted when Jahanara's questions tried to penetrate the mysteries of Khurram's 'reincarnation'. She was listening and writing her diary at once. Suddenly she stopped both and galloped into this cross-examination.

She closed her diary and put the pen back into the gold, emerald-studded inkwell that shone in the chamber's light. She wondered whether there was any need for such a simple thing as an inkwell to be so pompous. She thought it was the place in which things existed that defined simplicity or grandeur. She looked up and across the chamber, at Panipat sitting and reading beyond the curtains.

Poor man, of course—but also harder than a stone. How could this old eunuch put on the face of an innocent child, knowing everything and even being a part of the act? What he says is true, of course. It's the duty of hijras to guard secrets, failing which they would lose their heads. But how to extract the secret out of him, without him losing his head?—she pondered.

'Panipat, I don't want to get you into any trouble. I just want to know what happened that night. You know me, and know the reason behind my wish to find out the truth. Every word you utter will flow into my bloodstream as *amanat* and it will never emerge from there. No ocean could fathom my grief after I heard that Abba was dead. Why did they make me suffer? What was the reason? What was such an act orchestrated for? These questions have been tormenting me. Only your answers can save me from the torment. Won't you save me, Panipat?'

Panipat could never disregard this entreating voice. Women were inherently shrewd. They could move mountains using just a needle. They were the most cunning of creations invested with authority. Could a toy-clown like him ever raise his hat before Jahanara?

'I give up my pledge, Begum Sahiba. For you. You are my whole life. Can a slave disobey the command of one's own life? I will tell you. The mastermind of this act was Prince Khurram. There were seven actors. Your mother, the chief minister, the astrologer and the commander-in-chief played major roles. Sati-al-Nisa and the head of *bawarchi khana* played the supporting roles. This eunuch-slave of yours was merely a clown who tagged along.'

Panipat's speech was animated. His plump body shook as he spoke. He stroked his beard as he narrated the story, but his cheeks blushed. His kohl-lined eyes shone with mischief. Jahanara laughed looking at his gestures.

'Please don't laugh, Begum Sahiba. You are the genesis of this play.'

'I? What do you mean?' Jahanara was both shocked and irritated.

'Why are you getting angry with me? "You" doesn't exactly mean *you*. It was your dream. This play began when we tried to interpret your dream.'

The dream that Jahanara had described to Arjumand Banu at Kushal Khana and the results Abul Faizi, the astrologer, had predicted flashed in her memory. But how did it get tied to her Abba's act?

'The ties lie in the astrologer's predictions: the time is about to come when there will be a transit from Libra and Scorpio will be at its peak. Will everything happen on its own, Begum Sahiba? We have to make things happen, don't we?' said Panipat. The enigma of his words pushed Jahanara into a dilemma.

Abul Faizi and Khan Jahan Lodi had assured Prince Khurram that there could not be a better time to leave Nizam Shahi. They had two reasons. The first reason was Abul Faizi's astrological prediction that Scorpio was at its peak and so it was a favourable time to move. Secondly, Lodi had come up with a strategy.

Khan Jahan Lodi's spy brought the news that Emperor Jahangir, who had gone to Kashmir for rehabilitation, had passed away. He was buried in Lahore. Noor Mahal did not disclose the news, a clear sign of a conspiracy. Lodi suggested they reach Agra before the serpent encircled the throne. The current retinue wasn't going to be enough for the expedition. Asaf Khan and his regiment would help, but this was no time for battle. There was no one to claim the throne except Khurram, and there was no need for an invasion. The only enemy around was Noor Mahal. Would anyone wield swords to catch a snake? Couldn't a snake-charmer's pipe do that? The 'act' was such a 'pipe'—the need of the hour. It should be shocking and yet credible. Could there be anything more shocking than the news of the prince's death?

'What we witnessed in the tent that night was the first scene of the play. The prince spat goat's blood and fell dead. I entered the stage only after this first scene.'

Panipat went on with a description of a veteran actor. Jahanara found his narration both amusing as well as nauseating. Cool breeze wafted in, carrying the moisture of rain. A moth, with yellow eyes dotted on its black wings, came floating in the air. She shooed it away, but her eyes began to follow it, flying along with it. The insect flew above and sat on the edge of the jharokha. When another wave of the wind whirled in, it jumped and flew away, searching for the warmth of the wall lamp. A lizard's tongue, lurking behind the lamp stand, encircled the insect. Jahanara looked away. Panipat, who was looking at Jahanara from behind the curtains, laughed to himself, and carried on with his narration.

Banoori, Khurram's favourite elephant, was made ready with a howdah. It was spacious enough for two people to sleep on. Black curtains were drawn on all four sides. The coffin was kept inside the howdah. Arjumand Banu Begum sat guarding the coffin. Except for Abul Faizi and Karim Chand, others were asked to go much ahead of the elephant. This was against the customs. There was no shroud on the corpse. The queen should sit near the corpse's head, but Arjumand Banu Begum sat by its side. Those who should follow were forced to go ahead.

There was food and water inside the howdah. Arjumand Banu Begum opened the coffin and served food to the prince. Late at night, Abul and Karim Chand helped Khurram answer nature's call. On some nights, Prince Khurram himself got down from the elephant to give suggestions. They finally reached Fatehpur Sikri.

'You know the rest, Begum Sahiba,' concluded Panipat.

Jahanara was immersed in thought. The cold wind picked up pace and gushed in. A black feather dotted with yellow eyes swirled in it and fell on her lap.

It took a few more days for Prince Khurram's entourage to reach the palace of Agra from Fatehpur Sikri. Arjumand Banu Begum had everyone wait for an auspicious day to start the journey towards Agra, consulting a group of astrologers. Jahanara was surprised. How could faraway planets dictate the deeds of human beings on the earth? What was the need to wait for so many days?

There was another, less direct reason—the real one. Khurram had given orders to Asaf Khan to safely bring back his two sons from Delhi. He had also secretly sent a retinue of fearless soldiers as a backup to ensure that his sons came to no harm while being extracted. The wait was extremely tiring for Jahanara, who wanted to reach Agra as soon as possible. She was expecting to be reunited with her brothers Dara and Aurangzeb. Each day's delay caused her to wither a little more. She wandered in the harem and the gardens inside the fort at Fatehpur Sikri. She listened to the *surahs* and *hadiths* that Sati-al-Nisa taught. She spent quite some time writing her diary. However, stubborn Time refused to move along any faster, like an errant horse.

Jahanara played dice with the maids-in-waiting. They were hesitant to play with the princess at first. They were afraid to sit in front of her. But Jahanara insisted, 'Look, I may be the princess at other times, but at this game of dice, I am just your playmate. In a sport, every player is equal. Sit and play.' Yet they were hesitant. But after some days, as they played more and more, the maids lost their inhibitions. 'Roll the dice! Beat the piece!' they shouted in excitement. They fondly chided those who made wrong moves; they gently punched those who lost the pieces.

Somewhere within Jahanara, rose a sudden, sharp pain. A nauseating bitterness flooded her heart and mind, and a sense of loss clouted her body for a few moments. Would my world have been bigger, had I been a simple girl? Much brighter, exciting and free, perhaps ... she pondered. To hide her tears, she stared hard at the dice. Am I also being rolled like them? she thought with sadness. 'Roll two,' her opponent asked and Jahanara rolled the dice. The maids' shout of excitement cut through her sorrow and severed her bitterness.

'Here's two. It's you who won this game too, Mubarak!' the voices laughed.

Jahanara realised that it was she who had won all the games played so far. These were victories that could not be rejoiced. They had been given away by those who were slaves forever before the princess and her powers. She looked at the maids affectionately. Sati-al-Nisa's words flashed past her mind, 'With power, even an earthworm will gain the respect of a king cobra. Because of the seat it occupies. Power will grab things without asking and make you obey without telling.' A slight pride and arrogance rose in her mind, brushing aside these thoughts, and she looked up and sat erect. There was a tinge of sweetness in her saliva. She wondered if bitterness in its extreme form could turn into sweetness.

Arjumand Banu Begum said that they awaited the visit from the astrologers so they could select an auspicious day. Jahanara thought they were waiting for Dara and Aurangzeb. However, the news that Asaf Khan's spies brought that evening was unexpected, and unimaginable to all those present. Shahryar was dead. Had been killed, perhaps. His regiment fell before Asaf Khan's small regiment. Pulakki, whom Noor Mahal had appointed king last winter, had been beheaded. On Prince Khurram's orders, Noor Mahal was kept under house-arrest in the Agra palace.

CHAPTER 5

PANIPAT

The first rays of a winter's day touched the earth. Agra woke up to the beating of drums. The mosques in the Mughal territory offered special prayers during the *Fajr*, seeking blessings of the Most Beneficent and the Most Merciful for A'la Azad Abul Muzaffar Shahab-ud-Din Mohammad Shah Jahan. Special early morning prayers were offered at Hindu temples too. A few reluctant church bells tolled for the masses, while the doors of gurudwaras shut themselves, screeching grudges.

The person who had been Prince Khurram until last night turned into Emperor Shah Jahan, the king of the world, while Arjumand Banu Begum turned into Empress Mumtaz Mahal—expected but delayed transformations. At Khurram's age, Jahangir's kingship had been a year old.

Agra Fort was crowded with different kinds of people: foreigners, the representatives of the East India Company, the Parsis who were loyal to Shah Jahan, merchants, maulvis, Brahmins and artists as well as a few English doctors. The durbar was in a tizzy. There was a hullabaloo. The ladies of the zenana stood behind the curtains in the balcony, awaiting the coronation ceremony.

I was busy with a crowd of hijras. Jahanara gestured to me to come forward and I went.

She said, 'Abba the emperor and Ammi the empress—'

Before she could finish the sentence, I said, 'You are the princess of all princesses, Begum Sahiba. Please do remember this slave. It was I who coronated you first.'

A proud smile bloomed on her face, and she blushed. Mumtaz Mahal, who was sitting beside her, admonished, 'Jani!' and both of us became subservient.

Mumtaz Mahal's tone was different from that of Arjumand Banu Begum. It wasn't a tone but rather an echo—the echo of Noor Mahal. I registered this change with both surprise and fear. How quickly everything changed! History was just a long chain of the consequences of momentary changes. This change of tone was also a consequence, of things set in motion during Akbar's reign. Time was waiting in the wings, holding a consequence for what was happening today. But for whom?

Before my thoughts could march any further, drumbeats and trumpets were heard in the durbar hall. Jhanjs cheered the hall, Shenoys sobbed with joy. The torrent of the crowd's gleeful cries swept everything away. Emperor Shah Jahan stood at the centre of the hall, like a pink moon descended onto the earth. Petals of wishes were showered on him. Asaf Khan coronated Shah Jahan with the crown of the Timurid dynasty, the crown that had been worn by Babur, Humayun, Akbar and Jahangir before him. As the emperor raised his head, Asaf Khan stumbled for a few moments. Shah Jahan sat on the peacock throne, adjusting the crown on his head, which was askew.

Mumtaz Mahal had arranged a grand reception for the emperor in the zenana. Even though there were hundreds of maids and eunuchs in the harem, the empress had personally supervised the preparations. Her crisp appearance and gait never gave away her age or the fatigue of having given birth to thirteen children. The comfort and luxury that royalty entitled her to had rejuvenated her body and mind.

Jahanara was running alongside like a bright shadow of Mumtaz Mahal. Together, they looked like twins—with their attires and ornaments reflecting one another. However, something marked them apart: the content on the mother's face as opposed to the unfathomable longing on the daughter's. I understood what caused the difference between them: Mumtaz Mahal's arched stomach.

As the bawarchi khana wasn't big enough to feed so many, *shamiyanas* were erected outside the harem. There were hundreds of cooks, sweating on such a cold night. The air weighed heavy with warmth and cold—the warm aroma of varied dishes and the cold scent of perfumes. Mutton was being cooked in several copper vessels. A few ovens sweetened the air with the aroma of sugar syrup. Around five hundred vegetarian and non-vegetarian recipes had been followed. Mumtaz Mahal had given orders to avoid beef, as there were Hindus among the ladies in the zenana and the guests. There were several varieties of fritters and drinks. Prince Murad stuffed his mouth with a handful of samosas.

Jahanara chased after him, yelling, 'If you stuff yourself with this now itself, how will you feast on the rest? Go away.' Then looking back, she asked me, 'What are you doing, Panipat?'

I said, 'They are all cooking for the emperor and the empress. I am preparing *sherbat* for the honourable first lady of the Mughal Empire.'

'Jani!' She ran away, hearing Mumtaz Mahal's call. I followed after her, with a goblet of sherbat in hand.

The emperor came and sat on the marble stage set in a spacious shamiyana. Next to him was Mumtaz Mahal. When Jahanara and Roshanara fought to sit next to their father, the emperor hugged them both and but let Jahanara sit beside him, and moved Roshanara near Mumtaz Mahal. Murad and Shuja were already seated next to Mumtaz Mahal. Roshanara had to sit at the end of the row. I saw balls of fire in her eyes.

Almost all the family members were there, except Dara and Aurangzeb. Their arrival was still a few days away. 'Only they are missing the coronation ceremony,' wrote Abdul Hamid Lahri. The emperor had asked this traveller to write a book on his everyday activities. Even when the feast was on and people got busy serving or eating, Lahri was taking notes.

The feast got over just before midnight. Gifts from the attending representatives and personages had piled into a heap, and there was a similar one in the Diwan-e-Aam as well. All the guests left with handfuls of gifts. The ladies and hijras from the harem received gold jewellery, silks, muslins and gold coins. I got a pearl on Jahanara's recommendation. It was a huge white pearl with a grey crescent on it, a gift from beyond the Deccan.

'Aren't you a traveller? Tell us from your experience: what is this worth?' I asked Lahri.

'A pearl with a grey stroke is the rarest of the rare. The purest one—the signature of God Himself,' said Lahri.

That must have been true, or else would my Begum Sahiba have ever given me anything ordinary?

There was a separate palace for Jahanara within the zenana. It was small but charming and comfortable, with separate reading and music halls. There was a bathing chamber made of marble slabs, with mirrors hanging on the walls. A wide variety of flowers growing inside the palace spread the fragrance of their smiles. I was the only one permitted inside the palace, apart from Jahanara's parents, her brothers Dara and Murad, Sati-al-Nisa and her trusted maids. This enraged Roshanara.

'You permit this doddering old eunuch inside and chase away your own sister like an iblis. I will ask Abba to build me a more beautiful and bigger palace than this one. Then you try coming there, Jani, and watch how I chase you away.'

'Insha Allah, so be it!' Jahanara would say this so calmly that it never seemed like the equanimous answer of a seventeen-year-old to the bluster of a twelve-year-old child.

Roshanara would run away, tears falling like drops of fire. A few sparks of that ripened rage would bounce and hit me too.

Once after one such fight, Jahanara came near and pressed my shoulders. 'Poor little girl! She doesn't know the meaning of what she says. I seek your forgiveness on her behalf, Panipat.'

'Begum Sahiba, don't you know that I'm beyond joy and sorrow?'

'Time too. Why do you leave that unsaid?'

'Yes. Time also. But I didn't come here to listen to high praise. I came to tell you that Noor Mahal has come to meet Emperor Shah Jahan and asked to see you as well.'

Jahanara's face fell for a moment. 'Where is the serpent visiting him? In Kushal Khana or Diwan-e-Khas?'

'Neither. She is in Machili Bhavan.'

She looked surprised. The emperor generally didn't meet anyone there. If it was a public affair, he granted audience in Diwan-e-Aam. If it was a discussion with family members, he met them in Diwan-e-Khas. If he needed to consult anyone on a personal matter, the meeting took place at Kushal Khana. When Noor Mahal requested to meet him, he agreed to see her at a Diwan-e-Aam to be held in Machili Bhavan. It sent out the message that his stepmother Noor Mahal could no longer wield her earlier powers, and she got the message. No royal meetings had taken place in Machili Bhavan before this, and none did after this.

A chair was placed for Noor Mahal near the emperor's throne. But she refused to be seated and chose to stand. Behind the curtains of the balcony sat Mumtaz Mahal and the children, and in the row behind them were the concubines. It had been months since they had seen Noor Mahal with the reins of absolute power in her hands. So they were eager to pull apart the curtains and see her face once. When she heard the mild swishes of the curtains shifting, Noor Mahal turned around and looked up like a hooded serpent.

'Badshah Bewa, you may be seated. Tell me why you wanted to meet me. You need to be kept aloof for certain important reasons. But it doesn't affect my reverence towards you. You remain my father's beloved wife, the sister of the honourable Asaf Khan, Mumtaz Mahal's aunt, and the guardian angel of my soul. These bonds will never change. Neither will my loyalty towards them. I am duty-bound to give you a fair hearing. Please tell me.' The emperor's calm yet firm voice echoed through the hall. It wasn't clear whether it was due to the solemnity and the decorum of the meeting or the largeness of the hall but there was an aura of enigma to this scene. Everyone was enthralled by Shah Jahan's voice. The silence proved witness. I felt that his poise was coated with a tinge of mockery. Noor Mahal too must have sensed it.

'Fine, Khurram. I didn't come here to listen to your sugar-syruped words. They are sour to me. I don't think my powers were curbed by you, Khurram. You yourself know that you aren't capable of that. No fishing yard can catch an octopus. I am the one with a hundred hands, and I didn't come here for alms. Didn't you call me Bewa? I have come to claim what is owed to me on account of that authority.'

Hearing this, Mumtaz Mahal's face went red with rage. Jahanara grew restless, squirming at the edge of her seat. The emperor sat erect on the throne, unscathed by the stings of his stepmother. I slowly climbed down from the balcony and took cover in the darkness near the emperor's throne.

'Khurram, what I sought was a private discussion, between you and me. And you have made me stand before everyone and insulted me. Given the impure blood in your veins, you can only be expected to behave like this.'

No one had anticipated that Noor Mahal would utter these words. The heat of displeasure rose from all corners of the hall and converged at the centre of the *mandapa*. Asaf Khan stood up in anger, But the emperor's gestures sent him back to his seat. Unforeseen even by himself, Shah Jahan continued looking at Noor Mahal, a calm smile playing on his lips. But I could see his grip on the arms of the throne tightening.

I had stood witness when Noor Mahal uttered the same sentences for the first time. It was when Jahangir's second wife Taj Bibi Bilqis Makani had given birth to

Khurram, the male heir. We were celebrating the birth. I was the one who took the news to Noor Mahal. She declared that a *kafir* had been born into the Mughal dynasty.

Whether Akbar or Jahangir, there had always been Hindu women in the harem, as prostitutes, concubines or wives. Manmati, the princess of Mewar, was no exception. The whole world accepted her as Taj Bibi but for Noor Mahal. The kafir taunt 'chaunt' was an outcome of this.

'Badshah Bewa, it's a disgrace for me too to meet you here. I had intended to see you in Kushal Khana. A minute's delay in the time of appointment you had mentioned was the reason for this change of venue. My ministers were in a discussion with the representatives of the British Empire. This is important to me, for the future of this empire. If you are going to talk about the old days, I have no interest in that. It would be helpful if you kindly tell me what you expect me to do,' Shah Jahan said, crushing his rage.

'Khurram, I don't expect anything that is not rightfully mine. Didn't I tell you that I came to get what I deserve? Two things. One: I want the treasure of our dynasty, the Kohinoor diamond. And two: even if you don't agree, the fact is that I am the empress, and so a separate palace of my own is well within my right.'

Shah Jahan rose from his throne. The hall fell silent, all ears nervously awaiting his reply.

'Badshah Bewa, a palace for you will be built soon. Here. Near my own residence. Servants will be appointed for its maintenance. You can put your mind at peace as far as the palace is concerned. But you can't get the Kohinoor. It belongs with the emperor. It has been passed through one emperor's hands to the other for generations within the Mughal dynasty. This rare treasure is the symbol of our pride. I have the right to refuse this demand of yours, a right granted by Allah,' said Emperor Shah Jahan and left without waiting for a reaction. The audiences in the hall and the balcony also rose to leave. They dispersed making hushed conversations. Noor Mahal stood there, enraged—a tigress who had missed her prey. Someone from the hijras' group said later that she stood there without moving till the *Maghrib* namaz, and no one knew where she went after that.

CHAPTER 6

A month after the coronation of Emperor Shah Jahan, the palace was getting ready to welcome Prince Dara and Prince Aurangzeb. The Diwan-e-Khas had been renovated some days ago. New balconies had been built on all sides. The balcony at the main entrance was the highest one. It had a separate place for the emperor and the empress to sit together. The balcony adjoining the two walls was for the royal princes and princesses, and the rest were for the ladies from the zenana.

The royal couple waited at the new balcony. The restless eyes of their children were fixed on the entrance. Abul Faizi too waited for the auspicious hour when the princes would enter the palace. Jahanara was sure this was her mother's order. Mumtaz Mahal's belief in astrology went against Islam. Doesn't the Lord, who holds time, know the auspicious hour for us? Human deeds are timed by Him. Won't our faith in the magnificent God make every hour auspicious for us?

Three shadows appeared at the entrance: of Dara and Aurangzeb with Asaf Khan. Jahanara could see garlands of chrysanthemum flowers. Dara came running towards his parents with open arms. His was the joy of a bird, whose clipped wings had grown again. Hands folded behind his back, Aurangzeb walked as if he were carrying a huge, invisible burden.

Shah Jahan and Mumtaz Mahal embraced Dara and kissed his forehead, their eyes moist. Mumtaz Mahal held her arms open for Aurangzeb. But he reached only after her hands had begun to ache. An over-matured Aurangzeb bowed and said, 'Salam'. A disappointed Mumtaz Mahal withdrew her hands. When he bowed, his cap caught their attention. It was an ordinary, hand-spun cotton cap. They turned back as if they had forgotten to notice it when they kissed Dara on his forehead. But what adorned his head was a cap spun with gold threads, and studded with emeralds. Dara looked like a symbol of luxury and Aurangzeb, the metaphor for simplicity. Jahanara couldn't see much more than their perplexed faces from where she was.

Aurangzeb remained detached even when he met his brothers. He didn't have anything to say, even after so many years of separation. He said 'Salam' to everyone and moved away. However, Dara kept talking, as if to tell the tale of several days in a single breath.

The harem and the royal family moved to Fatehpur Sikri that evening. Panchmahal reverberated with the children's laughter. They jumped up and down in joy. When the call for the *Asr* prayer was heard, the shouts of cheer paused for a while, and then the waves of laughter returned. Amidst this uproar, Aurangzeb was on his knees, praying. After the prayers, he started writing in his notebook.

Jahanara asked, 'What is he writing, Dara?'

'Would he write a diary or poetry like you? He writes *surahs* from the *kitab*,' said Dara.

'What a good deed!' said Jahanara.

'Of course, it is indeed the only good deed in the whole world for him. He thinks eating, sleeping and playing are futile, and he believes that religious service is the only sublime deed. It's all very well that he believes in it. But I just can't stand it when he forces it on others,' Dara said.

'Aren't you exaggerating, Dara? He doesn't seem that overbearing or stubborn.'

Jahanara looked at Aurangzeb affectionately, who was putting the pages written so far into a leather bag. Then he wiped his face with both his hands and stood up. Aurangzeb, a pale figure, with a broad nose; there was dark hair sprouting under his nose and on his cheeks, and he was at a height that created the impression he wouldn't grow any further. He walked as if he counted each and every step he took. Jahanara kept looking at him until he descended the steps and was out of sight.

'Jani, what I say is as true as what you say. When we were taken to Lahore, he cried for the first two days. He would wake up crying at midnight and would sit in the darkness of the chamber and keep crying. He just didn't stop. He kept crying this way for more than ten days. He wet the bed in his sleep. Noor Mahal scolded him badly for it. Even after that, he wet the bed, and she threw him out of the room. He sat outside in the cold darkness until dawn. But the next morning, his face showed no signs of fatigue. From that day on, he was never afraid. He had learnt to face everything he was afraid of.'

Listening to Dara, Jahanara noticed the changes not only in Aurangzeb but also in Dara. The boy, who used to speak haltingly, groping for words, had now learnt to speak in a flow. His words were both argumentative and sweet. His appearance had also changed—he was tall and strong, his eyes were wide and feminine. His nose was sharp, just like hers and Arjumand Banu's, and under the thick moustache, his lips were thin and rosy. His determined gait could be likened to that of a wild animal, lurking to spring upon its prey.

'These boys have grown into men,' she told herself. One was at the peak of his youth and the other looked too matured for his age. She could no longer talk to them as she used to. It suddenly occurred to her that she should be cautious of Dara and affectionate towards Aurangzeb. However, unknown to her yet, the destiny that awaited her warranted that things be the other way round. 'Bhai Shikoh, what you say sounds more like a jinn story,' said Jahanara.

'I also thought so. But his actions that followed proved it to be true. When he was thrown out by Dadijaan Noor Mahal, left all alone at midnight, he was crying, frightened. A light, brightest of all the worldly lights, descended from the skies. Someone recited the surah: "Are you more content with worldly life than the afterlife? If so, know this. Everything except afterlife is trivial. If you don't walk the path of God, Allah will deliver you an agonising punishment." When the light vanished, so did his fear. He never cried after that.'

Jahanara wanted to talk to Aurangzeb, but whenever she approached him, he evaded her. He was always busy knitting skull caps or copying verses from the Quran.

On the day they returned from Fatehpur Sikri to Agra Fort, she went to meet him, taking Panipat along. Roshanara was standing at the entrance. She blocked the way with her hands when they tried to enter. To avoid a direct confrontation with Jahanara, she looked at Panipat and said, 'Tell your Begum that I have been instructed not to allow anyone inside.'

Her sharp tongue pierced Jahanara. Then enraged by Roshanara's snicker, Jahanara pushed her hand away. 'Do you have any idea whom you are talking to, Roshanara? I am Begum Sahiba. Do you have any doubts? I am here to meet my brother. Not you. Stay out of my way. I don't need anyone else's permission to meet him.' Jahanara moved forward. Roshanara held her hands again and pushed her backwards. Jahanara was about to fall, but Panipat caught hold of her.

'You devil of a eunuch, your Begum Sahiba may not need anyone else's permission. But you need the permission of the one whom you want to meet. Aurangzeb has given orders not to allow even the emperor and empress. Tell her that this applies to your Begum Sahiba too. Now take her away from here,' Roshanara said to Panipat, and then went past the entrance, flashing a venomous smile.

Jahanara clearly heard Aurangzeb's question, 'Who is outside?' and Roshanara's reply, 'No one. Two slaves went astray, but I chased them away.'

Jahanara stood frozen for a few moments. Panipat looked at her to check whether she was crying. No, she wasn't one to cry. Though her face looked like awilted rose. He heard her softly say, 'White Serpent!'

'Panipat, let's go,' she said. She walked away fast, as if she wanted to take refuge in a safe place before the shadow of humiliation devoured her. Panipat had to run to keep pace with her.

Jahanara swallowed the bitterness in private. Even when the emperor and empress asked why she looked so bereft, she hid the incident from them. She didn't have the heart to point fingers at Aurangzeb. But Sati-al-Nisa didn't have any compassion for him.

It was Sati-al-Nisa's responsibility to teach all the children. She greatly disliked it if even one of them was inattentive or distracted during class hours. But she couldn't admonish or punish them. She was also the personal maid of the empress, but could she punish the princes and princesses—no, she couldn't.

But she did admonish Aurangzeb, who was spinning caps during her classes. And he simply looked at her and said that all that she taught was vile and against the Islam. 'Why must a Muslim learn the Hindu puranas? Why should I learn about Hindu gods?' he asked.

'Don't you yourself think this question is inappropriate, Prince? Your Dadijaan and many before her were Hindus. Isn't your question a mockery of them?'

'I don't care about that.'

'Emperor Akbar himself said that we should know about all the religions and we should learn all the holy scriptures and art forms. Haven't you read it, Bhaijaan?' asked Dara.

'I don't agree with that.' Aurangzeb looked at him with disdain. Those words shook everyone. The reading hall fell silent. He threw away the book he had in his hand, took his leather bag, and was about to leave, when Jahanara held his hand and stopped him. Aurangzeb said in a stern voice,

'Jani, let go of my hands. You are also a dirty kafir. Why do you wear nose rings like Hindu women? Why do you dress like them? Why do you believe in their fake stories and eulogise them in your diary? Let go of me. Your unclean hands will defile me too.'

Jahanara let him go, wringing her hands as if to get rid of her disgust. As Aurangzeb left the hall, she muttered, 'white serpent', and scowled. When she saw Roshanara get up to follow him out, she cursed, 'An earthworm running behind a white serpent!'

Aurangzeb was summoned to Mumtaz Mahal's chamber. He repeated the things he had uttered in the study hall, only with more determination. The empress flew into a rage.

'Get out of my sight! I wish I had given birth to a serpent instead of you. It would have had some mercy. Ya Allah! I gave up five of the thirteen children I gave birth to. How come I suckled and raised *this one*?' she lamented.

Mumtaz Mahal's lamentation moved Jahanara. It also affected Dara, Shuja and Murad. But it fell like an empty cry on Aurangzeb and Roshanara's ears.

The royal couple and all the children were at dinner. The lively feast was accompanied by bursts of laughter. But deep in the minds of Mumtaz Mahal and Jahanara, behind all their laughter and joy, was a residue of the incident that had taken place in the study hall. It was evident from the way Shah Jahan permitted Aurangzeb to leave when he said salam after the dinner that Mumtaz Mahal hadn't reported any part of the incident to the emperor. Roshanara followed Aurangzeb out. Shuja and Murad took leave after a while.

Dara asked a question related to something he had read in a Hindu purana: 'Abba, is there such a thing as rebirth?'

'It is a complicated question. I don't have a ready answer for it. But many among the Hindus too don't believe in the idea of rebirth. Our religion says, it's just a figment of imagination. But at the same time, it says that the judgement will be delivered on the day of *Qayamat*. So, in that sense, both religions are aligned on the virtue of goodness. Both state that one should live righteously, do good, in the present birth, I believe,' said Shah Jahan.

Mumtaz Mahal laughed.

'Why do you laugh, Devi?' asked Shah Jahan, raising his eyebrows.

The way he addressed her descended like a lightning on Jahanara. The voice she had heard in her dream echoed in her ears now and called out to her lovingly. Her body quivered with ecstasy. She got a grip on herself, lest it betrayed her before everyone.

'I laughed at your diplomatic answer to Dara's spiritual question,' said Mumtaz Mahal.

'Akbar the Great dreamt of practising a spiritual politics. Am I not his heir? I will toil for his dream to come true. My heir Dara Shikoh will continue on the same path. His question and its background give me that hope. Am I right, Dara?'

Dara simply smiled at his father. Mumtaz looked at this and beamed with happiness. Jahanara gently held her brother's hand, and then tightened her grip slightly. When they took leave of their parents, on the way to their respective palaces, Jahanara saw two silhouettes under a chinar tree. One of them was Noor Mahal's, and the other, Aurangzeb's.

That night, she could not sleep in peace.

CHAPTER 7

PANIPAT

Navroz. The first day of the Parsi New Year generally fell closer to Emperor Shah Jahan's birth anniversary according to the solar calendar. His birth anniversary was celebrated twice a year. On the day which fell closer to Navroz and on his birthday according to the lunar calendar. A new addition was made to this ritual after he became emperor, as per Mumtaz Mahal's wish. A great fortune would be offered as gifts on the emperor's birthday. A large amount from the treasury and the granary would go to charity.

Closing the accounts on the coronation day, Abdul Hamid Lahri let out a sigh and said, 'I have travelled throughout Hindustan and beyond the Vindhya mountains. I have never seen such a huge fortune being spent on charity.'

'There is no such practice in other places! Didn't we loot and hoard everything here? Every grain offered here on charity was the fruit of someone else's sweat and labour somewhere. Every jewel given away today was drenched in someone else's blood. All this means nothing but wiping their tears with a silk kerchief,' I said.

Only after the words came out did I realise that I was being dangerously cheeky. What was this I had told the *Vakya Navis* of the durbar! I got nervous.

'Don't worry, I won't write this down,' Lahri assured me.

Perhaps he too was just like me—someone who was against power, but entirely dependent on it for survival. This was a dangerous predicament. One should either worship power or be against it. It is dangerous to get caught between the two. I wonder how I survived for three generations in the royal palaces amidst these perils. However, for power, both are the same. When needed, power will never hesitate to demand a sacrifice—no matter whether one stands 'for' it or 'against' it.

Large shamiyanas were pitched in the garden for the birthday celebrations. The emperor sat on one of the plates of a steelyard set at the centre of the awning. On the other empty plate, grains were first kept. Different grains equal to the emperor's weight were measured out and given to beggars, followed by clothes. The very wind blowing across the garden weighed heavy with blessings and gratitude.

Four soldiers came carrying a huge chest. The treasurer opened it and took out silver and other jewels from silk bags. He called out the names of important persons. The treasurer handed the bags to the emperor, who rewarded them to men who had been loyal to the empire. In the daylight, the faces of those receiving the gifts shone brighter than the precious metals. If what others got weighed as much as the emperor, what Khan Jahan Lodi received weighed three times more than that. I, who expected a three-fold brightness on his face, was disappointed to look at his vacant expression. His discontent was evident to none but me. It was like a lurking hyena.

A huge crowd had gathered in the durbar to wish the emperor on his birthday. The gaggle of hijras, unsatisfied with the new clothing and jewels they had received, quarrelled amongst themselves out of jealousy, eyeing what others had got. I left when someone informed me that Jahanara had summoned me.

Jahanara was esconced in her usual seat behind the curtains of Diwan-e-Aam. I went and stood close to her. She was unusually excited, and looked somewhat shy too. She, who usually sat ramrod straight, was on the edge of the seat today. Like a jinn on the edge of a merry dream.

'Panipat, can you see from here and tell me who is sitting in the left row under Abba's pedestal?' she asked.

'Begum Sahiba, my body may be old, but my eyesight is still clear. There are seven in the row you mentioned. I don't know everyone in the row. Can you point at the person?'

This was the right time to prove to Begum Sahiba that I, who was neither male nor female, could decipher a lady's heart quicker than any male or female.

My eyes scanned the row on the left. The first man in the row was a representative of the East India Company. The second one was the minister of the Parsi sultan. The third was a minor Rajput king. The fourth man was the son of the sultan of Turkey. I couldn't identify the rest of them. But I understood whom Jahanara's heart was seeking to know.

'Begum Sahiba, isn't it the third one you want to find out about?'

Jahanara's eyes widened in wonder, pierced me, wavered and stood still for a while. Surprised, she clamped her mouth with her hand. She asked in a deep voice, with her hands still on her mouth, 'How did you find out, Panipat?'

'There was no need for me to "find out". Your eyes betrayed your heart. Aren't they hovering over the third seat?'

She blushed. Her eyes became heavy as if intoxicated, her nose quivered, her lips seemed wet, her hands shivered, and she curled her legs around each other. She leaned back in her seat. When I sensed what brought about this change, remorse devoured me. Ya Allah, couldn't you have made me a woman, so that I could also have relished such ecstasy, even if for one moment? I fretted. Guilt overtook me the very next instant. Doesn't the Creator know who should be created and how? I don't know His reason for creating me this way. I may fathom it someday. I comforted myself thus.

'Begum Sahiba, the one whom you desire to know is Chattar Sal, the king of Bundi. A Rajput. He is related to your dadijaan Taj Bibi. Our emperor helped him to establish his rule. So he has great regard for the emperor and gratitude for the empire. He has come here on special invitation from the emperor. That's all I know. Can't the Begum Sahiba of this empire find out the rest?'

Even as she laughed at my joke, her eyes were fixed on Chattar Sal. He was talking to the emperor, but also seemed to be singing something amidst the conversation. Not a full song but verses, tuned to some raga. Jahanara turned towards me and gestured to me to bend down close to her ears. In a soft voice brimming with excitement, she said, 'Panipat, I know him already.'

I blinked. As far as I knew, she never left the zenana. Could she have seen him when her family went on a tour of the city? But this was the first time Chattar Sal was visiting Agra. It was impossible. Could she have seen him in the paintings painted by the palace artists? But I had seen all the portraits in the gallery, and this face was most certainly not among them. Where then did she know him from?

'Panipat, do you remember the dream I told you about when we were in Nizam Shahi? It was him I saw in the dream. It was this strong body I saw. It was this face that turned towards me like the sun turns towards a flower. It was these lips that came close to my ears and whispered a song. These were the very lips that kissed my forehead. It was him, who called me Devi.'

Her words were feverishly rapid and her voice fire-like. Her nervousness frightened me. Her excitement surprised me. She tried to say something else, but the claps from the durbar forbade it. The representative of the East India Company presented his gifts and was wishing the emperor. It was more of a list of demands than a birthday wish. If it was so boring to me, what about Jahanara, caught in all that excitement?

The attention she paid to the Englishman's speech revealed a desire different from her usual curiosity to know the proceedings of the durbar—a desire to prove something to someone. When I was about to talk, she silenced me. Dubashi was translating the Englishman's talk. The gist of the talk was that the British should be permitted to travel and trade independently in the territories under the Mughal Empire, which would be beneficial for both of them.

Jahanara pinched my hand and said, 'Ask him what the benefits are.'

I rushed to the commander-in-chief, Khan Jahan Lodi, and conveyed what Begum Sahiba had asked. He took the missive to the emperor. The hall echoed with the translation of the question in Dubashi's voice. 'Whatever be the demand, the British government will fulfill it' came the answer.

Jahanara sent me back with another question, which reached the Englishman, travelling via the commander-in-chief, the emperor and Dubashi: 'The British Navy should grant protection to our pilgrims to Mecca. Will that be possible?'

The Englishman raised both his hands as a sign of consent. The call of 'Allah Akbar' reverberated through the hall. Chattar Sal smiled, his gaze penetrating the curtains. A shy Jahanara lowered her gaze. She wanted to reciprocate the smile. And the moment she looked up, Chattar Sal raised his right hand in greeting. I understood that no veils or curtains could stop the words exchanged between two hearts.

Sati-al-Nisa complained to Mumtaz Mahal that Aurangzeb wasn't regular in attending the reading hours. But when Mumtaz Mahal asked Aurangzeb about it, he said he had no interest in Sati's lessons and he was learning what he ought to on his own. Mumtaz Mahal asked, 'How would you learn with no one to teach you?' The answer suffered no delay. 'Dadijaan Noor Mahal teaches me.'

'Sabbaash! A perfect teacher, the one who demands that mullahs and maulvis obey her command before the word of Allah,' said Mumtaz Mahal, lips pursed in contempt.

Aurangzeb rose abruptly, picked up his leather bag and writing materials, and left. He never came to the reading hall after that. He continued his study in his palace as well as in Noor Mahal's. He invited maulvis and learnt the principles of Islam, debated with the mullahs, and prayed five times a day without fail. He ate little, wore simple garments, spun caps and had them sold, offering the money earned to charity for the pilgrims. No one, except for Noor Mahal and Roshanara, was permitted inside his palace.

'His simplicity costs the government so much' were the words that escaped my inattentive tongue. Jahanara reprimanded me for that, a thing that had never happened before, and did not ever happen in the future. I understood my error when I pondered over it. To me, for whom luxury had become the 'normal' way of life—Aurangzeb, the one who had renounced it, seemed to be a laughing stock.

Dara Shikoh, on the other hand, was a connoisseur of the finer things in life. He was independent, calm and composed, and amiable to everyone. The absolute antithesis of Aurangzeb. Dara followed the Quran, but at the same time, he was interested in understanding other religions. Apart from mullahs, he also invited historians. It was Begum Sahiba who found it more beneficial. She knew more about the Hindu mythologies and puranas than a Hindu girl would. Her knowledge helped clarify many of Dara's doubts.

'It is neither the former emperors nor me. It's Dara—through whom the dreams of the great Akbar will come true,' Emperor Shah Jahan said one day.

It wasn't Dara but Jahanara whom this statement made immensely happy.

'It is true. Akbar's dream of a great empire is mine too. If I establish the Din-i-Ilahi that he wished to create, my dreams will also come true,' Dara announced after the class hours. Everyone except Roshanara said salam to him.

Overjoyed with pride, he told Jahanara, 'But, Jani, I will correct a huge mistake that the great Akbar made.

I will revoke the ban on the Mughal princesses getting married.'

Sati-al-Nisa said 'waah' in approval. Shuja and Murad blinked. Roshanara twisted her lips at first and said 'Sabbaash' after a while. Jahanara was shyly twirling her bracelets. When she heard the clear noise of gold, she looked down, blushing.

A dove glided down from the palace and sat all shrunk up in the jharokha's gap. It said, 'Ahem', as if to ask 'How are you?' Jahanara looked up and it fluttered its wings.

'Dara, you are right. But you begin to think about the yield even before sowing. Remember, Emperor Akbar did all these things after he became Akbar the Great,' said Jahanara.

Dara asked, 'You are right, Jani. Won't Abba and Ammi show me the way?'

Everyone smiled at Dara's cleverness, who made everyone dream what he dreamt. But Roshanara's face fell and she left muttering under her breath.

Time bade farewell to spring. The Yamuna was drying up, and her banks were visible. Nights were short and days lasted longer. There were heat waves even during the nights. Aurangzeb came down with fever. He was ill for more than a week but refused treatment. He refused to allow the royal physicians to enter his chamber. The English doctor sent by Mumtaz Mahal, too, was turned away right from the entrance. Aurangzeb wanted to heal through prayers and payers alone.

Jahanara and I went a few times to enquire about the well-being of the bedridden Aurangzeb, but Roshanara stopped us at the entrance each time and sent us back. Instead of feeling angry with Roshanara, I pitied Begum Sahiba. Who is she? A princess among princesses. The emperor himself depended on her wisdom. She would argue about Islam with the mullahs and could debate over puranas with the pundits. But she was ignorant as far as her own powers were concerned. I wasn't able to tell her this, but Sati-al-Nisa accomplished that.

'Begum Sahiba, you seem reluctant to think that women do not have political power. You aren't even aware of your own powers. We are hidden within our burqas. So what? Don't we hear and see everything? Can't you give suggestions to your Abba? Jahangir heeded Noor Mahal's suggestions. Abba consults you and your Ammi. Why should you hesitate when everyone else has accepted you as the Begum Sahiba. Your power is just like an arrow in the hands of an expert archer who hesitates to shoot.'

I saw the impact of Sati's words that very evening. Jahanara's fierce eyes made Roshanara move away, who had stopped her as usual. She went in like a shot arrow. I had to struggle a lot to hide my glee at Roshanara's fallen face.

Aurangzeb allowed Jahanara's visits until his recovery. An excited Jahanara told Mumtaz Mahal and the emperor that he spoke without any restraint. 'He is on a path of his own and he doesn't appreciate any intervention. Isn't that right, Panipat?' she asked me.

No. That wasn't right. It occurred to me that the 'path' would be paved over the heads of others. But I nodded just to comfort her.

During a night study, a nervous Jahanara told me what Aurangzeb had said to her in a conversation.

'Jani, our grandfather, Emperor Jahangir was known as the Conqueror of the World. When I become the emperor, I will be known as the Conqueror of the Universe. He was Jahangir, and I will be Alamgir.'

Jahanara was terrified when she heard this. How was it possible? According to the royal tradition, the eldest son had to be the heir to the throne. And Dara was the eldest, so he was the rightful heir to the throne. How could Aurangzeb, the fifth-born, claim the throne?

'But, Panipat, I saw the determination on his face when he said this. The fire in those eyes terrified me,' she said. Jahanara never went to his palace after that.

CHAPTER **8**

Only spring and summer are meant for human beings—when the long days make nature pay heed to human beings. The sun prolongs the days only during these seasons. It drags the day and hands it over to the night, without the heart to part with it. Winter doesn't know love. It drives away the sun like a slave, shortens the days and drags the boredom of nights. Jahanara found winter rather monotonous. She liked long days.

There was so much to do in the longer days: Sati-al-Nisa's classes, Abba's durbar and chess with Ammi, lunch with everyone, discussions on Islam and other religions with Dara, listening to the secrets of the zenana from Panipat. She could listen to music in the garden till the stars winked in the evening. The boredom began with nightfall. The cold didn't allow anything, except sleeping and staying awake and listening to the murmur of the night lamp till the dawn.

Jahanara told Panipat about her distress after the Maghrib namaz that evening.

'Your complaints surprise me, Begum Sahiba.' Panipat smiled, narrowing his eyes. Wasn't it surprising to hear this from someone who dreamt as much as she did?

'Dreams are weapons to defeat boredom. The Creator blessed only human beings with these weapons. What for? Wasn't it to realise one's own self and others? Those who refuse to understand others, see their own selves in their dreams. Time is a burden only to such people. Those who realise their own selves will reveal themselves in others' dreams too. For them, dreams are wings. So those who are born to be emperors and empresses never have the chance to get bored.'

Jahanara, who was listening carefully to Panipat's words, burst into laughter at the last sentence.

'What you say now is more surprising, Panipat. You address me as an "empress". Me, who can never ascend the throne of power. This is strange.'

Panipat was silent for a moment. His eyes followed the slave who came in with a small torch and a jar of oil. His eyes were pinned on her until she lit the lamp and left the chamber. The light from the torch she held high lengthened her shadows as she walked away. In a few swift steps, both she and her shadow disappeared. Stroking his beard, Panipat turned towards Jahanara. Jahanara looked at his wavering eyes.

'Begum Sahiba, this is what's happening inside you as well—this play of shadows. You hold up your dream's torch like that slave, and so, the shadows of ennui fall ahead of you. Bring your dreams forward and the shadows will disappear. When your dreams illuminate your deeds, these shadows will vanish forever. Begum Sahiba, addressing you as the empress is not mere empty praise. This is how I really see you. May the Creator forgive me for prompting Him—he already knows what should be done and how. But I couldn't help thinking this way: had you been a male child, wouldn't the whole empire have been under your control? And so what if you are a girl? The emperor himself depends on your counsel. You are blessed with a luck that your mother Mumtaz Mahal and your grandmother Noor Mahal were not blessed with at your age. Asaf Khan waits on your opinion. Mullah Shah Badakhshi proudly says to the emperor, "What spiritual wisdom she has at this early age!" Dara, the emperor-to-be, follows your suggestions. What else do you need, Begum Sahiba? For me, you are the empress, even if you don't wear the crown and sit on the throne.'

Panipat got busy untying the knots in his beard, with his eyes narrowed, as if the talk was over. Jahanara was watching him. His face stiffened and reddened, and he kept sticking out his tongue along with frequent sighs. 'A peculiar creature, this Panipat,' she told herself. 'This peculiar creature knows me better than I know my self. Even Ammi doesn't know so much about me. Is it because he has been with me since the day I was born? One's changing appearance and physical growth may be obvious to someone else, but how can one's mind—'

'I have a seventh sense that aids me in reading the minds of others, Begum Sahiba.'

His eyes shone from the satisfaction of unknotting his beard. Clapping his mouth shut clownishly with both his hands, he said before Jahanara could speak,

'The reason for your boredom is not the cold season but your age. Amidst other dreams, you should realise, you have another recurring dream, which can't come true. That is what has been troubling you. A surprise from the emperor awaits you tomorrow.'

He walked towards the door, then descended the steps, ignoring Jahanara's voice, which chased him: 'Tell me what it is!'

'You devil!' she said, with a hint of anger but immediately corrected herself. He didn't reveal the surprise just to keep me excited, she thought. He knows I will think about this throughout the night. Ammi might tell me what it is. But she must be waiting for Abba to visit. Didn't Panipat say I dream of something impossible? What could that be? What does he mean by 'a problem of age'? Jahanara pondered, swarmed by guesses of all sorts.

As the curtains flapped, a cold wind blew into her room, carrying the fragrances of roses, jasmine and kasthuri strewn in the garden, the frankincense sprinkled on the incense bowl, the sandal burning in the fireplace, of the *agil* from the zenana, and of the incense sticks burning in the mosque. Jahanara's eyes went wide, and with a deep breath, she tried to inhale all the fragrances. She took it all in, differentiating each and every smell. The chain and wall lamps were burning fragrant oils too. Her memories echoed Mullah Shah Badakhshi's words.

'All the lights descend from one divine light. All the noises emerge from one single sound. All the rivers flow from a single source: the river of mercy. All touch is the touch of a single embrace. All fragrances rise from a single ocean of fragrances.'

Then the wind fell silent and the room turned cold. She heard the call for the Isha prayer. That call had a divine fragrance, mixing in all the great fragrances she had just smelt. She got ready for the prayer.

Shah Jahan had plans to establish a new capital in Delhi. The empire would spread wide—from the summits of the Himalayas till the edge of South India. Such an expansive kingdom couldn't be ruled from the fort of Agra. An even bigger capital was warranted. Delhi could be made the nerve centre of this vast empire. Emperor Shah Jahan was determined. New buildings, palaces and gardens were needed. Armouries, prisons, stables and bazaars too.

Shah Jahan was so possessed with the idea of establishing a new capital that he forgot about food and rest. On certain days, he even postponed the durbar, didn't visit the Kushal Khana, kept away from the *mushairas*, missed going to the art gallery. He stopped sitting in the library or in the living room, and avoided his wives as well as the hospitality of concubines. For days and nights on end, he remained immersed in the plans and maps drawn by the royal artists. But what he didn't neglect, despite this preoccupation, were two things: praying five times a day and sleeping in Mumtaz Mahal's arms.

Along with the artists in the palace, there were sculptors and architects from different regions of Hindustan. Artists from Persia, Gandahar, Constantinople and European countries also enjoyed the emperor's patronage at the Agra fort. People swarmed the palace corridors throughout the day. The aroma of different cuisines rose from the bawarchi khanas.

Jahanara and Mumtaz Mahal were with the emperor in the Diwan-e-Khas when the plans for Delhi were finalised. Dara, Murad, Aurangzeb, Shuja and Roshanara were also present. Asaf Khan, the commanders-in-chief, ministers, the loyal Rajput kings and minor kings, jagirdars and zamindars were in attendance. Abul Faizi, too, was there. Mullahs, historians, Vastu experts and astrologers had also been invited. Behind Shah Jahan's throne, close enough to hear everything being said, sat Abdul Hamid Lahri, with an open book.

The debates were on. The hall was astir with voices at different pitches. As if a flock of birds had perched under a banyan tree for a rest. But the low voices were silenced when the emperor cleared his throat. All eyes came to rest on him. Shah Jahan rose from his throne and made an announcement.

'In the name of Allah, the most gracious, the most merciful, I, Shah Jahan, the fifth emperor of the Timurid dynasty, declare this before you. We have decided to change the capital of our empire. The new capital will soon rise on the banks of the Yamuna. It will be hailed as the gem of Hindustan. Just like the river, the city will outlive Time itself. Everything is available there. There is nothing that cannot be found there. May Allah shower His beneficence for the birth of such a city.'

After the announcement, he left the hall through the back entrance. Mumtaz Mahal and others followed him. Shah Jahan's walk had an unusual pace today, and a majesty never seen before. Others had to run to keep up with him. Reaching the Kushal Khana, he sat on his bed, looking pleased. 'I have never seen you walk this way even while heading to the battlefield,' said Mumtaz Mahal.

He admired the playfulness in her tone. Beaming with pride, he agreed, 'You are right, Devi.'

'I feel prouder of this than I did of any of my victories in the battlefield. People easily forget the victories and defeats faced on the battlefields. It is bound to be forgotten. But buildings? Isn't it an art form? Won't it last forever? I want to live forever, Devi. That is why I am so excited. More than an emperor, I will be happier to be known as Mumtaz Mahal's beloved and the worshipper of art.

'What a way to talk in front of your grown-up children!' she said, blushing with shyness.

Two soldiers brought in a large screen, stretched on a teak frame with engravings. This was the proposed capital city's portrait. Shah Jahan rose and walked towards it. His eyes shrank and then went wide, as if they were examining an intricate painting. His eyes lingered on the screen for a few moments. The others came and stood behind him. Their eyes following the emperor's eyes.

The buildings were painted small on the screen. Red buildings. Pathways with trees were painted green. Ponds were painted blue. Barracks were painted brown. Settlements were the colour of burnt sand. The fort ramparts were a deep shade of saffron. And at the centre, stood a mosque, completely white.

'This is the mosque I am going to build in Shahjahanabad, our new capital. A prayer hall as chaste and flawless as a full moon. I have even picked a name for it. I will reward the person who guesses the name right.' Shah Jahan turned and looked at the expectant faces. His eyes rested on Jahanara's face, whose lips were murmuring, 'So, this was what Panipat left untold.' The shadow of a riddle clouded all the faces, except Aurangzeb's, which had on it indifference and disdain. Shah Jahan was taken aback by this for a moment, but put on a smile.

'Abba,' said Jahanara. 'Shall I answer?'

'Jani, if your answer and my choice are the same, I will give you what you want.'

'Aren't they the same, Abba? What you're saying you will give me and what you have already decided to give?'

Between nods of amazement at her cleverness, Shah Jahan's eyebrows rose with a question: How did she guess?

Mumtaz Mahal thought: The secrets of the harem do not always remain secret. Someone loyal to her or Panipat must have told her.

'Both are one and the same, my dearest daughter. I have already decided. The new city will shine with your artistic skills. This is the reward for your answer. Tell me.'

Jahanara closed her eyes and raised her hands in the air, as if in prayer. 'It's He who created me. It's He who guides me on the right path,' she uttered these sentences and paused for a moment. She said, 'Moti Masjid', as if uttering a musical note without making a mistake. She asked, 'Isn't this the name you have in mind?'

'Mubarak, Jani!' said Shah Jahan, embracing his daughter and kissing her on the forehead. His eyes brimmed with happiness. Mumtaz Mahal hugged her daughter from behind and drew Jahanara's head close to hers. A happy Dara raised his hand and said salam. Aurangzeb and Roshanara were looking keenly at a moth swarming the chain lamp at the entrance.

'You may create anything you desire in the new city. Land will be given to you. You may build anything you want there. Madrasas, galleries, dance halls. Anything you like. You will get the funds and artists you need for that.'

Caught in the swirls of ecstasy, Jahanara was lost for words. She took the emperor's hands and said affectionately, 'So, this was the reward Panipat had been hinting at. What a priceless reward! None of my siblings were granted this gift. This shows Abba's love for me. For this love alone, I will live as his shadow. Allah, bless me with this boon.' Her body shivered in ecstasy. Mumtaz Mahal gripped her shoulders.

The dinner was arranged in the Kushal Khana. Apart from the royal family members, other important guests had also been invited to the dinner, which was unusual. The aroma of food and wine wafted on the evening breeze.

While dining, Jahanara shared her dreams for the great capital city. Shaded pathways with parks and gardens on either side. A spacious quadrangle with shops where all the pathways reached. A pond brimming with moonlight, Chandni Chowk.

'Jani, I am doubtful if people will remember me. But you have already made plans to remain unforgettable,' Shah Jahan teased Jahanara.

'Who will remember me alone, Abba? None of us would be here without you. I might be remembered when *you* are remembered, just like the stars are noticed only alongside the moon. Let's not talk more about this. I need the emperor's permission for something. Do I have it?'

'How can I grant permission without knowing what you need permission for, Begum Sahiba?'

'Permission to conduct a *shetkhani*.'

Surprised to hear this, Shah Jahan looked at Mumtaz Mahal, and she lowered her eyes, blushing.

Shetkhani was a fair meant for young lovers to meet and exchange hearts. It was a 'love bazaar'. Shah Jahan was surprised that his daughter wanted to conduct the fair. He looked at her. Blessed with beauty and brimming with youth, she was at an age that made one too stubborn to yield before reason. She was no longer a child. His mind at once felt close to her and distanced from her. 'As you wish,' he said.

Roshanara's was the first voice of approval, even before the emperor said yes. Jahanara thought, she will be on my side soon. And Aurangzeb too. But Aurangzeb flew off the handle.

'Jani, where did you get this idea from? Women should be patient, calm and modest. Do you want this market to degrade yourself? Aren't you ashamed? You're a disgrace to Islam!' Fuming, he hurriedly left the hall, as if walking on burning coals. Both the sisters stood outside the Kushal Khana in the freezing cold, Jahanara murmuring 'white serpent', and Roshanara confused whether to follow him.

CHAPTER 9

PANIPAT

Aurangzeb insisted that the emperor revoke the permission he had granted for shetkhani. It was against Islam. He argued that it would mislead women. Hearing his arguments, Jahanara began to fear that her father might repeal the permission. She dispatched me to spy on the discussions between the emperor and Prince Aurangzeb over this.

'Panipat, his intentions are not to safeguard the religion but to deny us our liberty. We should never give in.'

'Aurangzeb, the women won't be disgraced because of a fair conducted merely for amusement. Can anyone put out the sun just by sprinkling a glass of water on it? This is simply an occasion they want for a little bit of merriment. My predecessors never forbade it. Nor will I. I also enjoy looking at the cheerful faces. I spent the whole of last year crushing the Rajput rebellion. I am tired of recalling the fallen faces, the battle-stricken men and the bomb blasts. I want to see my subjects on the streets, their faces beaming with happiness. But I also want to see you happy. I suggest two ideas, which may make you happy. Let us all go to Fatehpur Sikri for Salim Chisti Urus. And I would like you to get involved in the construction of Moti Masjid in Shahjahanabad.'

Aurangzeb stood spell-bound, defeated by the emperor's shrewdness. He bowed down as if accepting defeat. When he took leave, the emperor repeated:

'Sultan Aurangzeb, had the fair—which you have such a strong objection to—not been there, you wouldn't have been born.'

Aurangzeb lingered for a moment at the door and then left with a smile as the emperor's message finally hit home.

When I said this to Jahanara, she let out a cry of joy, 'Sabbaash to Abba!' and clapped her hands in happiness.

'Panipat, you know why Abba said that. Tell me, please,' she fawned.

She would feign curiosity, as if she were hearing the account for the very first time. At the time, I hadn't the slightest idea that this was the beginning of a story that would have the entire Hindustan in thrall.

The nine-day shetkhani fair was held at Meena Bazaar. It was a festival for young royals, in which the women from aristocratic families gathered. The shopowners and customers both were women. The things sold by or to them were also meant for women: heaps of dresses, ornaments, cosmetics, oils, balms and perfumes from all over the empire and beyond. Girls too came from these places where the commodities were sourced, to participate in the fair.

There was talk about these girls everywhere—on the streets, in the palace corridors, the harem and the zenana. These talks were a feast for the fourteen-year-old Khurram's ears, who was eager to unravel one of the most difficult riddles of the universe. He was pestering me to take him there. None of my tricks to evade him worked. Finally, I agreed on one condition: he was not to reveal that he was a prince. If he agreed, I would take him there. And he did agree.

Khurram was too tall for his age. His gait unconsciously betrayed the pride of a recent victory in the battlefield. I was afraid it would put him at risk. But the innocence that shone on his face reassured me to a certain degree. We managed to go to the stalls without facing any hurdles. Women spoke with us without hesitation. A few of them stroked Khurram's newly sprouted beard. The more mischievous ones toppled his turban. One or two even pinched his cheeks. Khurram's twinkling eyes and blushing cheek betrayed the ecstasy he was immersed in. However, a fifteen-year-old girl selling Parsi silk towels, pearls and attar recognised him as the next heir to the Mughal Empire. They came face to face. It was as if Khurram's heart had been searching for her all along, and now, with nothing but a thin screen between them, Arjumand Banu had ended the search. I am the body and you are my soul. None will say that you and I are separate.' At the time, I didn't think of it as anything more than a senseless blabbering, but the truth was that I was witnessing the lines coming alive.

Shah Jahan said, 'I came to buy the most valuable thing here.'

Arjumand Banu said, 'I am the most valuable one, but you cannot buy me.'

'There's nothing I cannot buy. I can pay the huge sum required to buy the whole fair.'

'That huge sum won't be enough to buy kajal for my eyes.'

'Even if I give the gems, pearls, gold and silver lying in my palace treasury?'

'They will just diminish before my smile. There is no value for a commodity that is not genuine.'

'Will it be sufficient if I give the fortune of the whole city?'

'That won't be worth even the grace of my walk.'

'If I surrendered the wealth of entire Hindustan?'

'They would be mere glow worms before my body's radiance.'

Arjumand Banu's pride in her own beauty annoyed me, but there was no trace of anger on Khurram's face; what was there was an unquenchable thirst to gain what had stolen his heart. He moved away a little and said, 'Panipat, she is the most beautiful woman I have seen until today and will ever see hereafter. It is not just the beauty, did you notice the confidence on her face and the wisdom in her words? Her beauty gives her such confidence and wisdom, perhaps. Or are her confidence and wisdom the reason behind her beauty? Whatever may be the case, but she is going to be my wife. Nothing can change that.'

I wondered how a boy as young as him, who hadn't touched the threshold of adulthood yet, could speak with such conviction. But then if he could win a battle at fourteen, this too was possible.

He went back and stood before Arjumand Banu. 'I offer myself as the price. Is it a fair price?' Pushing behind the heir to the empire and the gallant warrior who won battles, Khurram had transformed into a poet who worshipped beauty.

The screen shifted for a moment, and Arjumand Banu's face flashed like a lightning. From behind the screen, she said, 'If this is the price you are offering, I too am ready to offer myself to you, Prince A'la Azad Abul Muzaffar Shahab-ud-din Mohammad.'

Surprised, Khurram looked at me. I lowered my head. How could I be made responsible for something I didn't know about?

Emperor Jahangir didn't pay heed to Khurram's wish. Royal weddings weren't happy endings of the love stories of princes, but rather tools of expansion of power. They were equations based on political calculations. Emperor Jahangir had done some calculations for Khurram's wedding too. He had given his word to the Parsi king that Khurram would marry his daughter. That was the primary duty of a Mughal prince. Arjumand Banu could surely be his concubine. But he was too young for that. He ought to wait.

'Panipat, do you think it was Emperor Jahangir who said this? Surely all of it is Noor Mahal's trickery.'

'I will wait. I say this in the name of Allah—she is the one who will be my wife. I will do anything for her. But I will honour the emperor's word too,' Khurram fumed.

And he accomplished it. He waited. And when he turned eighteen, he married Gandhari Begum on his father's insistence. It was a political alliance. In Khurram's parlance, a new addition to the slaves of the zenana. I was the happiest when Khurram married Arjumand Banu, but I shed tears in secret for Gandhari Begum's misfortune.

Khurram brought Arjumand Banu Begum to the Agra Palace and announced, 'Here is the light of my life. She will be the light of this palace too. My Mumtaz Mahal.'

I saw Khurram's face, which was usually like an eclipsed moon, shine like a full moon. I saw something else too. The chain lamps, wall lamps and the moon at the window, which heightened the brightness of the white marble walls and floors—everything paled before the new bride. As Mumtaz Mahal entered the palace, Noor Mahal's face lost its light.

The arrangements for the fair were being made. Items to be sold were heaped at stalls, and the ladies started coming. The royal path and midways were crowded with people, their chatter could be heard all over. The palace guards and soldiers rushed to the barber shops.

The ladies in the harem guarded the henna shrubs. Hijras were bargaining with attar merchants.

'Panipat, everything is in your charge,' Jahanara told me. Roshanara repeated the statement, albeit as a warning. I felt sorry for the girls. Poor souls, no pleasure, except for this false happiness, would ever be theirs.

The first three days of the fair passed like a festival. On the third day, Jahanara asked everyone to gather for dinner. The ladies and eunuchs hiding in the shade of the zenana, the heat of the bawarchi khanas, or in the dampness of the laundry hall, joined the celebration, laughing and bantering with abandon. It was a celebration of liberty.

Roshanara came searching for us, followed by her maid. There was a big silver vessel and a small brass vessel in her hands.

'Jani, your favourite *julab mosdh*, prepared specially for you.' She emptied the silver vessel into a goblet. The drink flowed into the goblet, an overwhelming smell of fruits and roses rising from it.

'Panipat, this is for you.' The maid brought the brass vessel close to my face. The bowl had gulab jamuns floating in sugar syrup.

Roshanara stood there, with a soft, enticing smile on her face. She waited till Jahanara had finished the drink and I had eaten the gulab jamuns. Then she walked away with her servant in tow. She walked into the darkness past the awning. I could see a white shadow moving amidst the trees. The shadow then moved away, while Roshanara stealthily disappeared into the awning. I wasn't sure whether to share my suspicion with Jahanara, and finally decided against it.

Jahanara set the goblet down and rose. But as soon as she stood up, she fell back on the chair. She rose again, her legs unsteady as if she were wading through water. I was confused and nervous. What she had been made to drink was clearly not just a fruit juice.

'Panipat, have you noticed the change in Roshanara in these past few days? She is so pleasant with you as well, isn't she?' Jahanara slurred as she said this. She began to walk but stumbled. Holding her hand, I took her back to her palace. I was careful that no one saw Jahanara in this state. The one who used to run like a rabbit was now walking like an arrow-struck swan. As soon as we reached the door to her bedchamber, I collapsed with a stabbing pain in my stomach.

When I regained consciousness three days later, I found myself in a dark room in the zenana. 'They said your food had been poisoned. What special recipe did you secretly swallow?' one of the eunuchs asked scornfully.

'Shut up, you devil!' I shouted.

I saw a shadow at the door: Jahanara. She came closer and held my hand. 'I was so scared for you, Panipat.' Her eyes brimmed with tears.

'I won't die so easily, Begum Sahiba. There are a few more days left for me in Allah's treasure, and he will never let me down.'

I went to the fair that evening, and took charge of it again, even though Jahanara had asked me not to. But my body couldn't keep pace with my mind. I sat down exhausted.

'They used you as a pawn to defeat me. May Allah punish them!' said Jahanara.

I laughed at this. Sweeping my gaze around the fair, I noticed that Roshanara was nowhere to be seen. There was no sign of her at the fair in the last few days. Poor girl, I thought her guilt was unnecessary. She was merely an arrow, the bow was in Aurangzeb's hands. Begum Sahiba also knew that.

CHAPTER 10

PANIPAT

Celebrations were shortlived. News arrived in Srinagar that riots had broken out in the Deccan yet again. Taking advantage of Emperor Shah Jahan's absence from Agra, the Marathas had reared their heads again.

On receiving the news, Shah Jahan told his retinue, 'I expected this to happen, but not so soon. Commander Khan Jahan Lodi is there. He will handle this.' An experienced war strategist, Khan Jahan Lodi was highly skilled at mustering a strong defence. Shah Jahan had reassured everyone, yet a niggling suspicion gnawed at him. On his orders, the retinue commenced its journey from Srinagar back to Agra. During their journey, the second piece of news, confirming his doubts, arrived. Khan Jahan Lodi was marching towards the south with a cavalry of seven thousand soldiers. An elephant battalion further bolstered the army. An attack was expected, but betrayal was not.

'You should've foreseen this too,' said Mumtaz Mahal. She was right. But Shah Jahan believed that

Khan Jahan Lodi would never betray him. He was his childhood friend and they had grown up together. Above all, they were related on his mother's side.

Emperor Jahangir had sent Khan Jahan Lodi to suppress the riots in Gandahar. Unable to tackle the people of Gandahar who fought fiercely for their motherland, Khan Jahan Lodi had had to return defeated. Infuriated by his failure, Emperor Jahangir had driven away Khan Jahan Lodi. Forbidden from stepping into the empire's territory, Lodi roamed about like a refugee on the boundaries for years. When Shah Jahan ascended to the throne, he brought him back and appointed him as the Amir of the Deccan territory.

Khan Jahan Lodi had forgotten gratitude. Reinforcing the rebels with the Mughal army under his command was worse than joining hands with Bijapur's sultan. All the enemies of the emperor had come together in a huddle, and Amir Khan Jahan Lodi had helped them. Was the support he had shown all these years false? Had he feigned loyalty all the while secretly planning a revenge? It was more important to crush the betrayal than putting down the Marathas' offensive.

When he returned to Agra, Shah Jahan called Dara to Kushal Khana for a meeting. Aurangzeb was purposefully ignored. Shah Jahan decided to lead the regiment himself. He ignored Mumtaz Mahal's objections. He was like a meteor burning with anger.

Jahanara was happy that Dara had been called to the meeting but uneasy that Aurangzeb had been ignored. Aurangzeb himself didn't seem to care. However, Dara, chosen for the battlefield, was hesitant. Jahanara knew the reason behind this reluctance. Nadira. The girl Mumtaz Mahal had chosen for him. Going to war meant missing the opportunity of getting to know her. But duty awaited the prince in the battlefield. A section of the infantry and cavalry marched towards the Deccan territory, and the emperor's retinue was getting ready to follow.

The tradition of going to the battlefield with family and relatives had been started by Shah Jahan. Merriment, wives and concubines were necessary there too. He brushed aside the objections, and came into disrepute. But this time, things were different. Mumtaz Mahal was pregnant. Murad's marriage had been fixed. Work on the new capital was underway. There were sparks of discontent in the Bengal region. The East India Company, which had enjoyed Jahangir's support, was fast spreading its roots.

'Must you lead the regiment when we are mired in all these other crises? Won't the Mughal flags and our commanders be enough to rattle the enemies?' Mumtaz Mahal tried to dissuade the emperor, but Shah Jahan denied her points furiously.

'Devi, your words surprise me. You know the circumstances well. This isn't a battle against enemies but traitors. It's time for the Bijapur sultan and Khan Jahan Lodi to see who I really am. By missing this opportunity, I will be triggering the fall of the Mughal empire. If I allow this to happen, won't my ancestors hold me to account for throwing away the empire they captured and expanded?' As if Shah Jahan stood in the battlefield—which grew larger and larger in his imagination—his words got fiercer and fiercer.

Then cooling down a little, he said, 'As you said, the Marathas are not the kind of enemies who will shudder looking at the Mughal flags. Theirs is a regiment of devils who believe they were born to battle. What they do cannot be called battle but a barbaric trick, of attacking unpredictably from nowhere. Therefore, I should lead the regiment to foresee and outmanoeuvre their tricks. If what I know of the Marathas is right, they will be the end of Timurid dynasty. If I don't lead from the front, Mughal history will never forgive me.'

In the next few days, the emperor's unusually small retinue marched towards the Deccan territory. Though he half-heartedly asked Mumtaz Mahal not to accompany him, Shah Jahan knew that she would not stay behind.

Mumtaz Mahal's retinue comprised her maids-in-waiting, an English nurse (as per the royal physician's suggestion), Jahanara, her consorts, Panipat, the group of slaves and hijras under him, concubines, some cooks and their servants for running errands, wagons carrying food and clothing, palanquins and howdahs for the royal women, a cavalry of five-hundred horses, an infantry four times bigger than that, elephants and camels to carry munitions, and hound dogs.

The retinue looked like an uprooted city on the move. The dust flying up from the movement of thousands of feet swirled in the air. Birds flying around lost their way in the cloud. The panic-stricken faces of the common people turned dark.

Dara Shikoh was leading a section of the infantry. Shah Jahan was at the forefront of different regiments every day. Enthused by the emperor's company, the regiment marched full steam ahead. The retinue followed behind slowly since Mumtaz Mahal was in a delicate state.

Not only had the riots rattled the Deccan territory but also nature, which weighed heavily. Parched lands saw no rains for years in a row. Paddy fields appeared like mirages. Cows and buffalos sniffed about the sand, looking for hidden grass roots. Scorched by the hot sun, the rocks and mountains made the nights unbearably hot. Jahanara was shaken up one day by what she saw from the howdah.

Two men came running, chasing after a bony cow. The cow managed to get away, but the men stayed behind, rooting in its dung with a stick. One of them picked up something and bundled it in his upper cloth. The other shouted and then assaulted him. The beaten one howled and hit back. What he had bundled fell out and got scattered on the ground. I was walking close to the elephants. I went and separated the two men. Frightened, they ran away.

When they stopped for lunch, I explained. The men had fought for grains. With no cultivation possible in the drought-affected lands, people suffered without food. They swallowed anything edible, struggling to assuage hunger. Driven to desperation, they even gathered the undigested grains in cattle dung.

After learning the reason behind the scuffle, the morsels Jahanara had eaten refused to go past her throat. The golden bowl she held weighed heavy. She thought the ghee rice in her bowl stank. Jahanara stood up and quickly moved away, fearing that her burnt intestines would spill out of her mouth. It occurred to me, albeit at the wrong time, that hunger is the god of all Gods.

All along the route to Berhampur, we saw not human beings but starving statues. They extended their hands towards our retinue and begged for food. Jahanara asked the pantrymen to give them food. The pantrymen were hesitant. 'How can we give away food when what we are carrying is insufficient for our own selves?' Jahanara argued with the emperor, 'Are you going to build the empire defeating those dying from hunger?' She growled at Dara, 'Have you forgotten Mu'in al-Din Chishti's words? Be with the poor,' she lamented. 'Why does God punish human beings?'

Soon, Jahanara realised that others valued her words, which reflected their love for her. She lay her head in Mumtaz Mahal's lap and wept. On the emperor's orders, some of his representatives rushed to Berhampur and returned with bundles of grains. Watching this, Jahanara was moved to tears.

'Begum Sahiba, what kind of tears are these? Tears of joy?' I asked with a tinge of mockery. Jahanara didn't know.

Shocking news poured in one after the other. Khan Jahan Lodi had joined hands with the rioter Jhujhar Singh Bundela. Other Maratha rebels had also joined them. The Mughal regiment was aghast. The soldiers' camp was three miles away. It became clear to the emperor: this was not going to be an easy war. It had to be won with tactics, and so he changed his battle plan. He decided that reliable commanders, Khan Dharvan, Abdullah Khan and Sayid Jahan Bara, would lead the regiment. The cavalry would go first, followed by the infantry. Between the two, Shah Jahan inserted a rifle brigade.

Shah Jahan knew Khan Jahan Lodi's strategies: infantry first, followed by the rifle brigade, and then cavalry at the rear in order to chase and kill those who escaped the first two. Shah Jahan thought this change in strategy would work. However, the enemies' plans were vastly different this time: they would launch an attack from nowhere and disappear before the opponent realised what had happened.

With such a war strategy, defeat was certain. The emperor was deep in discussion with Dara and the commanders. When he arrived at a conclusion, Jahanara saw her father's face clear up and gleam, which reminded her of his time in the Deccan. The retinue wasn't stationed away from the soldiers' camp. The night reverberated with the trumpeting of elephants, the neighing of horses and the barking of hounds. The snatches of conversation carrying over from the soldiers' camp sounded like secret codes. And amidst these sounds could be heard Mumtaz Mahal's groans. She was in labour. Jahanara couldn't sleep a wink.

Is giving birth really so painful? After bringing thirteen babies into this world, hasn't Ammi become used to the pain? And what's the reason for bearing such pain? Her love for Abba? Is love painful? Yes, his love is painful. Why else would he make her die so many deaths? Did Ammi, like the foolish wife of Kalava Rishi in Hindu mythology, think that her virginity got renewed after each delivery? Should a woman lose herself for the sake of her loving husband? Does a man deserve it? What am I going to lose? And for whom? No, the opportunity won't arise. Akbar's restrictions won't allow for it. Abba cannot defy the edict. He may not want to. Why does my heart still yearn then, knowing everything? Whose voice is it that repeatedly calls me Devi? Why do my heart and body feel a thrill when I hear it? My body melts and my heart flies. What kind of despair is this that no one but I know?

Jahanara was staring at the flame of a lamp, lost in thought, and didn't hear Mumtaz Mahal from the next tent for a while. When she became aware of her surroundings again, she ran guiltily. Mumtaz Mahal was sitting on her bed. Pain and fatigue had weakened her voice.

'Jani, did you see anything outside?'

She hadn't, for she had come running. She parted the curtains and looked outside. The darkness thickened with white smoke. Balls of fire rolled away. Meteors sprang. Silhouettes of horses galloped. The air weighed heavy with heat and the smell of char. She heard the heavy stamping of elephants' feet and the loud cries of humans. She turned back in fear.

A smile overshadowing the pain shone on Mumtaz Mahal's face. 'The Timurid strategy has brought victory to your Abba,' she said.

Jahanara was confused. The Timurid strategy?

'Yes. That's what Khurram has used. This battle will be over soon.'

'I don't understand, Ammi.'

The commanders had used an old technique to thwart the enemy regiment. Hay straw had been spread all over the ground in a circular area, and caltrops buried under it. As soon as the opposing army advanced, the soldiers mounted on horses had thrown down torches from outside the circle. When the hay caught fire, frightened horses and soldiers ran away and fell on the sharp caltrops. The soldiers then set fire to the haystack on the bullock carts. The panicked horses and elephants killed their own soldiers, while the Mughal soldiers killed those who fled the circle. By the end of the night, the enemy regiment had scattered and vanished.

When it dawned, nothing except for smoke hiding the clouds, dead bodies and abandoned weapons, was left on the burnt and charred land.

Khan Jahan Lodi had fled the battlefield. 'Till the time the traitor is alive, victory is incomplete,' said Shah Jahan. That meant they could not leave the Deccan territory for the time being.

Jahanara felt a vacuum inside her.

The emperor declared Berhampur as the Deccan's capital. This was announced in other parts of the empire too. 'I cannot escape this wretched land until Shahjahanabad is built,' Jahanara grumbled.

'It's not just you, Begum Sahiba, I can't leave either—can I?' I said.

'Oh! What's it to you? You are an independent creature.'

'Isn't it a mockery to call someone who was a slave for ages independent? Everyone is a slave in one way or another—to people, emotions or power. Only when we become conscious of the "slavery", we think of liberty. Do the slaves bought and locked away in the harem know they are slaves? Do the concubines brought by the emperors—Akbar, your grandfather, your father—have the slightest knowledge of their slavery? If they come to know, won't the palace be set ablaze?'

'You confuse me, Panipat? What are you saying? That slavery is happiness?'

'Not at all. Slavery can never make anyone happy. Except, of course, when one is slave to God, the One with immeasurable grace and unfathomable love.'

Jahanara pondered over my words. Only that one learns on their own endures, not what others teach them. Jahanara learnt things by going within.

The Berhampur palace was refurbished to suit its new status—the capital city palace. Merriment began. The ministers and other important officials arrived from Agra. Aurangzeb, Roshanara and Murad came along with them.

The durbar hall, harem, zenana, separate rooms for the princes and princesses, the emperor's sleeping chamber and the entertainment hall—everything had been made ready. The mosque built by Akbar was renovated. Two more rooms were built inside the palace for Mumtaz Mahal to rest in. A special bath chamber, more spacious than the other rooms, was built for the expectant queen's bath.

I was there with Mumtaz Mahal, when she delivered all thirteen children. I had never seen her so weak.

It was an unusually hot day. The air was parched. The day lingered on. As the sun set, the hot sigh of the mountains descended over the land. I saw the hakim and the maid servants running towards the bathroom. I followed them. The emperor and Jahanara stood panic-stricken. Mumtaz Mahal had fallen on the floor. The nurses and maid servants laid her on the bed. Her face turned pale. Her eyes were fixed somewhere else, they could not recognise the emperor or Jahanara.

The bed was taken into the hamam. The emperor left, his steps drained of energy. Jahanara stood close to me. Her trembling betrayed her fear. Maid servants ran in and out of the hamam.

'Panipat, once when they said that Abba had died, I pleaded to Allah, and Abba was returned to us. When you were poisoned, I prayed and you were saved. I will pray for Ammi. She won't leave us, will she?' Jahanara asked me piteously.

Before I could answer, she began to pray, her invocation sounding like a melancholy tune. 'Allah, you are my saviour. You created me. You guided me on the right path. You can end my life. You can revive me. I ask for your blessing, O Gracious One.'

No one slept that night. The emperor anxiously went and stood at the door to the hamam. Then he paced outside restlessly. People came from the tents, one after the other, enquired about the empress, and left. Astrologer Abul Faizi and the Hindu scholar were arguing, looking up at the sky and turning the pages of the books in their hands.

Only when a cry from the hamam shook me back into senses, I realised that I had fallen asleep standing. Jahanara was with Mumtaz Mahal. The maid servant from the *hamam* told me that the princess had called for me. The light of the palace lay diminishing on the bed. Shah Jahan's beloved was gasping.

Jahanara was sitting on a small stand near the bed. Mumtaz Mahal's left hand tightly gripped her daughter's hand. This was perhaps the first time a daughter was waiting on her mother's delivery. Jahanara's face had a mature expression. While Mumtaz Mahal's shrunken face had the look of a fearful child. Allah, what a sight this was! Hakim was giving instructions to the servants from behind the curtains. 'Ask the empress to open her legs. Has she done that? Right. Now ask her to hold her breath and push ... Do you see the baby's head? No? Ask her to push harder. What? Don't you see the head? The baby has turned. Ya Allah, what an ordeal!'

Mumtaz Mahal shouted in spite of the pain. 'I can feel the weight easing out of me. Are you going to kill me right now?'

'Hakim, she is bleeding heavily. What to do now?' asked one of the maid servants.

'We cannot do anything without taking the baby out. Both of you hold the empress's legs and push them towards her stomach ... Do you see the baby's head now? Pull it out ... Is it a boy or a girl?'

Mumtaz Mahal let out a loud cry, and the maid servant's voice answered, 'It's a girl.'

Dawn was still an hour away. The stench of blood and torn womb hung in the hamam. The maid servant laid the newborn near Mumtaz Mahal. Jahanara looked unblinkingly at this creature with the smell of birth. Mumtaz Mahal's tired hands touched her daughter's hands.

Mumtaz Mahal's final cry and the maid's scream were heard together. 'What?!' Hakim panicked.

'The bleeding hasn't stopped.'

'Make her lie on her back.'

I ran to the bed to help the maid. A small pool of blood had stained the bedsheet. Mumtaz Mahal's body shivered once and then froze. Hakim held out a small bowl from behind the curtains.

'Panipat, make her drink this.'

Pomegranate juice with opium. I gave it to Jahanara and she fed it to the empress. As the juice passed through Mumtaz Mahal's lips, she fell asleep. Poor Jahanara was still in shock.

Light dawned in the east. Mumtaz Mahal opened her eyes and said, 'Jani!' Jahanara looked tenderly at her mother, as if she were the mother, and her mother the child. 'Abba?' she murmured. Only when Shah Jahan parted the curtains and went near the bed, did I realise that he had been there all this time.

'Arjumand!'

Mumtaz Mahal's face lit up. 'Khurram, I am leaving you. She will take care of you on my behalf.' Her hands rested on Jahanara's hands. And then they didn't move. Ammi, Arjumand, Badshah Begum, Empress—Mumtaz Mahal didn't hear any of the calls. After the *Zuhar* prayer, her body was put to rest in the *qabar* on the banks of Tapti.

PART II

CHAPTER I

JAHANARA

My life is a broken crown with its pieces still intact.

My soul, a discoloured leaf, tossed about in the storms and rains. The blue light from the heaven shines through the patterns of its veins.

Every mosque is a prison. So is every palace. Those who walk the path of God can conquer the world.

Who are we? Just particles from the past? Sown with a hope of sprouting in the future? I, one of such particles, write down my thoughts.

I want to untie my diary. No. No. Why should I? This book—my only companion in this imprisonment—written in the blood from my wounded heart.

I write these lines from Agra Fort, in the dim light of a candle. My hands shiver. I bury my thoughts in the depths of secrets. How else can I live? Am I not a woman? But, here, on this lonely night, I can sing my sorrows to 'forgetting'. I can narrate the story of life only to 'forgetting'.

The sun sets. The wind rises. The earth breathes the fragrance of flowers. Here, at Anguri Bagh, every flower evokes a memory. The flowers on the way to the dining hall look like the flames of lamps. These are the very same flowers I got the garlands for my brothers' weddings strung with. These purple ash flowers fill me with sorrow.

The musical instruments fall silent at Diwan-e-Aam. But the evening weighs heavy with a melancholic tune. I smell the fragrance of red roses as I remember Dulera's songs. Touched by the tunes, my thoughts float away to an imaginary world—beyond the walls of the fort. I call Chattar Sal 'Dulera'. His music takes me to untrodden worlds. His face is unclear in my memory, but his voice constantly rings like a song in my ears.

When I was in my Delhi palace, I was just like a butterfly in Shalimar Garden. A butterfly that searched for nectar just to forget the evening's impending darkness and death. I was just one among the butterflies with bluish-green wings and golden pollens shining on them. Ascending the ladder of sunrays, butterflies escaped the rising evening stars, which snuffed out their brightness.

When I saw Dulera for the first time from behind the jharokha in the durbar, I was a little girl. I was stunned. He went near the emperor's throne and greeted Abba. Who was he? A reincarnation of Nala, the king of Nishada? Did I write to him just like Damayanti? I dedicated my being to this Rajput. No one had defeated me before him. No one will after him. My heart became his at the very first sight. He became the emperor of my soul on that very day, and still is, to this day.

Now, I waited for him in the palace garden. Won't he come soon? Won't he come to save me, when all the swords of Hindustan have been sharpened to defeat us? No lady would have given him bracelets like the ones I am going to give him today, I thought.

I heard his greetings from beyond the curtains—destiny's wall between us. I stood up to greet him back and thanked him.

'Must you thank me, Badshah Begum?'

Through the curtains, I could see his eyes, as bright as the sun and as deep as the sea. The sun had painted his white turban gold. The pride of victories held his head high.

'Your honourable father has come to Udaipur at this time of crisis. To show our reverence towards him, we established a pillar-lamp and the flame is still burning. The flame will remain alive till the last of the Rajputs lives. I will wield my sword to save your honour.'

I pressed my lips into the gap in the curtains. 'What about your own honour, then?'

The smile on his lips vanished.

'This Hindustan is a cursed land. We kshatriyas and brahmins spoiled it long ago. Do you remember that Rajput blood runs in your veins too, Begum Sahiba? The brave Samar Singh of Mewar went to the battlefield to save Delhi and Ajmer from Mohammad Ghori. In the dark of night, he saw a veiled beauty. She lifted her veil and said, "With you, Hindustan will also be destroyed." Delhi was defeated, centuries ago. Now, the pride of Hindustan is gone too. We, who should save Hindustan's holy mountains and rivers, are fighting against our own people for power.'

'Your king Prithviraj fought for Samyukta, the princess of Kannauj. Do you remember what she told the king when he was getting ready for battle? "Dying a brave death is to live forever. Think about immortality. Hack the enemy into pieces. I will wait for you as your wife on the other bank of the river." When the king died, she prepared to commit sati. Before climbing into the pyre, she said, "I will meet my beloved in the realm of the sun. Not in this Yoginipur." Do you believe that death unites those who cannot be united on earth?' The single question contained everything I had been longing to ask for years.

A smile, which lit up his face, became his reply too.

'The tongues of fire in the pyre purify the soul. It is a riddle. Fire sets the body free from all ties. The soul finds the heart it belonged to—either in this world or on its journey in search of God.'

There was a surge of joy within me. I walked towards the curtains. Won't these curtains fall, the way a fortress surrenders itself before those who lay siege to it? I shuddered with happiness. I groped for words to veil my shyness. He stood with an enticing smile on his lips.

Who could change what destiny had pre-ordained for us? Who could change the course of stars?

Dulera said, 'A prophet was meditating under a tree in a dense forest. The curtain obscuring his face so far vanished that day. We suffer, fight and die for nothing. Begum Sahiba. Emperor Akbar saw just one thing. He realised that there was nothing behind the curtain. All the voices are the voices of one. All the colours are the colours of one. All the lights are emanating from one supreme source. The one who said this was the real emperor of Hindustan.

'Your ancestor, Akbar. He was able to restore the Eka Linga temple. He was able to place the Quran on the pedestals taken from the temple. An outsider, he wielded his sword against us, of course. But he was also the one who opened the doors of our own homes for us. He placed Hindus and Muslims on the same plane. This country's freedom shattered with the end of our Maharana Pratap Singh, whom Akbar was never able to defeat. But through Akbar, a new path opened for Hindustan. Until the pride of the Timurid dynasty and Akbar survives, the descendants of Rana Pratap Singh will stand by his dream. I swear on the sword my ancestors held high. I dedicate my soul to you, Emperor Shah Jahan and Prince Dara.'

He raised his sword and its brightness glowed around his head like a halo.

CHAPTER 2

JAHANARA

The sky had never been so close to me as it was then—a crystal-clear canopy of blue stones above the earth. The earth turned into a dining hall, the stars into chain lamps, the flowing water into the music of sitar and flute. I invited the whole universe to share in my happiness.

I sat near the throne of nine gems—the throne of Emperor Shah Jahan. All the princes and the important people of Diwan-e-Aam were also present. My beloved Dulera walked in silently with his head held high. All the other faces turned pale just as the stars turn dim when the moon rises. The imaginary garland in my hands fell around Dulera's neck. The voices in the hall rose, sounding like the rustling of leaves. His name was announced. I looked at nothing but his eyes. I was always looking at those eyes—deep as the ocean and bright as the sun—to guide me. A woman without her husband was just like a day without the sun.

I dreamt on, sitting in my balcony. Fireflies danced in the air, like the torches in a wedding procession. Shaykh Ibn-al-Arabi explained how men realise their dreams with determination. I wanted to write a letter to Dulera about this. I wanted to unravel my secrets through words chosen carefully—just like the facets of a chiselled diamond wrapped in silk are slowly uncovered. Dara would revoke Akbar's law after he ascended the throne, defeating his brothers. He would hand his sister over to her groom and also her powers to him.

I wrote. But the night turned red. The sun that rose from the sea turned its redness into gold. The garland on my lap withered. Beyond the Feroz Shah stream, a group of merchants passed, chasing the camels away. Their pace revealed their determination to complete the day's work.

Sitting in the balcony, I filled that night with thoughts. I translated them into a letter and sent it to Dulera. Naseer from the palace brought Dulera's letter, which I wanted to read without anyone's knowledge. I was reminded of an ancient mosque near the fort, and I stood up to go there.

Shivering with excitement, I climbed up the dilapidated steps. The strong smell of wild resins made me drowsy. The rusty voice of a magpie robin invited me. There was a hermit sitting on a deerskin mat. It was a strange sight, a Hindu hermit at the doorstep of a mosque. A coconut shell and a staff lay near him. He was chanting, 'Only a fool would look for immortality in the physical body. The body is just like the leaves of a chinar tree—short-lived and ephemeral, like the foam of the sea.' I dropped some coins into his coconut shell. His blind eyes pierced me, as if looking into my future. He held the shell in front of me and said, 'Take back your gold coins. Why are you searching for happiness outside of your own soul?' he asked. He threw the coins on the ground and walked away.

I went near the well to read the letter. Every word reflected his nature—generous but simple as a child.

'My salams to you. If you become Samyukta, I will become Prithviraj, and I will lay siege to Kannauj. My beloved, my world turned into a garden of roses reading your letter. I remembered what Samyukta told her lover. "We women are ponds, you men are swans. Who are you, if you part from our bosoms?"

'I was overwhelmed by your letter, crowned by your blessings. My salam to you. I strode forward with your reward, as if in a victory procession. The birds sang just for me. The pelicans greeted me with their long beaks. Whatever flew in the sky and crawled on the earth knew my happiness.'

Beyond the road lined on both sides with tall cacti, amidst the cassia trees with coral red flowers, was a ground, spread wide like the sea. The blue sky above was like a spider web amidst spring's greenery. I wanted a palace to be built right here, a palace with thousands of towers.

In my life there hadn't been a happier day than this one. Even the poor folk looked happier. What else are we going to own except this? Here, a woman carried a water-filled pot on her head. Her brass pot shone brighter than the emperor's gem-encrusted crown. Her smile revealed her teeth, brighter than the pearl string around my neck.

Shahjahanabad was a wonderful city. I wished to build huge inns here. Spacious and beautiful. There could not be a city in Hindustan greater than Shahjahanabad. The travellers coming here would go back refreshed. My name would never be forgotten. But I would use gold only to help the poor.

To give my camels some rest, I got down in the large courtyard before the fort. My dreams rose just before my eyes. Words could never express my happiness— the happiness I relished when I realised my dream.

Chandni Chowk had turned into a place where people from all over the world met. Roads from Zanzibar, Syria, England, Turkey, Khorasan, China, Kabul and Turkestan came all the way to Chandni Chowk to witness its splendors. There were pomegranates, grapes and watermelons in the fruit shops. Flower shops turned the earth into a bowl of fragrance. Attar in thousands of bottles, with a dream in each bottle. Everything was bought and sold here. The hullabaloo from everywhere echoed like the different lines of a poem. Astrologers here suggested solutions to the problems of men and women. Here, a lady, covered in a white robe from head to toe, was just asking about her future. Then she disappeared into the crowd. Oh astrologer, you, who knows the language of the skies … Tell me what destiny has written for me in your book? Perhaps the planets and stars have nothing to shower over me but grief.

Mansabdars, amirs and kings went to the durbar with their retinue. The regiment's march echoed the beats of the battle. Another crowd went to Diwan-e-Aam. Dancers arrived in silk-curtained palanquins. Elephants moved towards the zoo, wearing silver bells around their necks and tassels made from the fur of Tibetan cowtails. Meddling with their majestic walk, baby elephants ran along playfully. Tigers followed them. Bengal cheetahs. Caged eagles. Though they were caged, they were the messengers of our empire, of the skies. Hounds from Uzbekistan. Everything was beautiful, of course. But the deer that arrived at the end of the procession epitomised all beauty.

The procession moved on, in sync with the roar of trumpets and the beats of drums. The images flashed right past my eyes. But there was one abiding image in my restless mind: a victorious Dulera dismounting his horse.

I was dying to see him, the one who would be wielding his sword along with Aurangzeb. I longed for his arms to embrace me …

I keep living and breathing these dreams for days. When one reminisces about the past, they see it anew in a different light. The palace, which returns to my memory each time I think about our first meeting, is no longer in existence. There's no garden either. River Yamuna's music cannot be heard from there. My garden is being planted far away. No dilapidated mosques there. A new mosque of marble stone rises. The Jumma mosque that Abba is building for me. My poor old mosque disappears behind the shine of marble.

My favourite dancer Gul Bai performed a new composition in the Kushal Khana for me. I brought her from Gwalior to learn dancing from her. She was my teacher and my fellow dancer. No, not just that, she was also a close friend to me. Her dancing never failed to enchant me. Not once did she close a performance unrewarded.

Gul Bai danced, covered in jewels gifted by me.

A truth dawned on me that day: there was no dance without the dancer. Tansen's music lived on even after him. Amir Khusrau was no more, but his ghazals had survived. Payag's paintings would remain even if Payag was no more. But if Gul Bai was no longer here one day, there would be no dance. She and her dance were inseparable. When I realised this, I looked at her more affectionately.

> The fragrance of the jasmine in my courtyard pervades
>   my chamber,
> My love, I wrap my letters to you in this fragrance,
> No answer comes back from you, none at all,
> Yet, the jasmine in my courtyard continues to bloom,
> Its fragrance still wafts past my bed.

Gul Bai danced to the tune of this ghazal. The melancholy of the song echoed within me. Melancholy spread on Gul Bai's face too. But it was not the melancholy of the song, it was the sign of an impending doom that I saw on her face. I felt restless. Gul Bai left after the performance. I followed her out.

There were red and blue glass lamps on either side of the corridor. I called out, 'Gul Bai!' She turned and looked at me, and in that moment, a disaster struck her. As she turned around, a lamp's flame caught her upper garment. In sheer panic, she ran away like a deer caught in a wildfire. I ran after her. Both of us rushed out of the corridor and into the palace's courtyard. I removed my shawl and covered her with it, trying to put out the fire. The fire, which caught her attar-soaked garments, leapt onto me as well. I screamed. The Diwan-e-Khas was in session. Hearing our frantic cries, many ran towards us. Was Dulera among them? Would he touch me? Or, would someone else touch me, right in front of his eyes? Would he stand idle? The flame of disgrace was fiercer than the fire that had scorched us. Gul Bai collapsed to the ground, taking me down with her.

CHAPTER 3

JAHANARA

I am writing after a long time. Unable to hold the quill, my hand shivers. My vision is blurred, as if my eyes are layered with smoke.

'Allah, with your grace, I survived. But will I be crippled? If that is my destiny, undo my existence,' I pray. My pleas didn't miss His ears. He, whose grace knows no limits, whose love is unfathomable, saved me from the abyss of death. He didn't let me down. He makes me write. His grace showers on me like rain from the heavens. In the rain, my parched body comes alive like rejuvenated soil.

I was bedridden for more than two months. Unconscious of the days and nights. Whenever I regained consciousness, I would be writhing in pain. When I opened my eyes, I saw the fierce flames of fire; when I closed them, a smoke-filled darkness engulfed me. Gul Bai's last cry kept ringing in my ears. I was unable to lie on my side. I had pus-filled blisters all over my body. A body that had never known the odour of sweat had now turned into a stinking bundle of flesh. Whenever I screamed at the peak of my pain, Hakim gave me something to drink. It tasted familiar, and it pushed me to a point of no pain.

One night when thoughts dawned clear, I realised that I wasn't in my palace. I recognised the place when Nadira came near me. I was in Dara's palace. My loving brother was taking care of me. If he came to power, everything would be all right. Dara knew me better than Abba. When I thought about this, my eyes became moist. 'Begum Sahiba, you have crossed everything you had to cry for. Why these tears now?' asked Nadira, wiping my tears with a towel dipped in rosewater. I noticed a change in her beauty—the beauty of carrying a life within. Nadira was talking, sitting by the bed. I heard none of her words. She let out a fatigued sigh of joy. I was thrilled, as if I were looking at Ammi. Dara's wedding had taken place without Ammi.

I was reminded of an afternoon on the banks of Tapti, six months after Ammi's death. The Deccan sun was burning hot as if it were the day of Qayamat. Trees stood still, as if they had forgotten to breathe. Animals licked their own sweat to quench their thirst. Birds were too weak even to flutter. Between the banks of the great Tapti, water and mirage looked alike. The Tapti, which used to flow fiercely, seemed to crawl now, cursing. Whom was it cursing? They said that Tapti was a male river. It seemed as if the river was reprimanding—'You wretched creatures! You let the beauty of world wither under the sun.

'Son of the waters, Emperor Shah Jahan takes her away, for he doesn't want any other male breath touching Arjumand Banu Begum. He wants her to listen to her friend Yamuna's murmur, not your male voice. Yamuna, whom she listened to for fifteen years. A temple of love, which was built for her, chiselled from his dreams, awaits her. He awaits her.'

Abba could not stay in the Deccan without Ammi. When there were no signs of immediate riots, we returned to Agra. Aurangzeb brought Persia in the north under his control. He was capable of ruling the Deccan too. Abba made him the governor of the Deccan. When he was coming towards the south, our retinue was heading towards the north. We spent one night with him. He shocked and surprised me. He was so simple. Attired in the most ordinary way, he looked like a fakir. But his body, walk and words betrayed a flamboyance contradictory to his simplicity. The humility he displayed in front of the emperor was just a show.

Abba returned to Agra a changed man. A senility set in and hastened to defeat him in a matter of months. There was melancholy in his eyes, which became inseparable from him very quickly. Weighed down by memories, his back was bent. His majestic walk slackened.

'Abba, you are shrinking into nothingness,' I said one day. He looked at me for a moment and then his eyes returned to staring at the marble memorial rising beyond the windows. 'Jani, there is no Khurram without Arjumand Banu Begum. Don't you know that?' he asked, without looking at me.

'You are not just Khurram, Abba. You are A'la Azad Abul Muzaffar Shahab-ud-Din Mohammad Shah Jahan Badshah, the head of the Timurid dynasty, the emperor of the Hindustan. If you become so aloof, this empire will be crippled. Power is not just an ornament, Abba. Isn't it a responsibility? And you are trying to relinquish it making Ammi the reason. If Empress Mumtaz Mahal were alive, she would have said, "Your Abba shouldn't feel my absence." She asked me to take care of you, and I intend to keep my word. Forgive me if I am wrong.'

I said this and bowed before him. Abba rose and stood near me, smiling. He took me in his arms, and whispered—'Devi'. It didn't feel like a father's embrace. There was no affection in the whisper, but a quest. Since I started living in a separate palace, so many years ago, Abba hadn't touched me. But that day, my body and soul felt the male touch and the anxiety concealed in the way he had addressed me as 'Devi'. For a moment, I faltered, mistaking Abba's embrace for Dulera's, and his calling me 'Devi' for Dulera's caress. Then, I freed myself from his arms.

Throughout that night, I lay awake, thinking about Abba, about Ammi, the bond between them, and about Abba's other queens and concubines. Ammi wasn't the only woman Emperor Shah Jahan knew. There were other wives. Akbarabadi Mahal, Qandahari Mahal, Hasina Begum Sahiba, Qudsiya Begum Sahiba, Fatehpuri Mahal, Sirhindi Begum Sahiba and Manbawati Baiji Lal. The stepmothers I could name. But there were innumerable women locked in the harem, whose names it was impossible to remember. What was the name of the relationship Abba had with these women? He may have married them for political reasons; still, they were human beings, were they not? Ammi possessed something that was missing in all of them? I wondered what he got from them that fulfilled him? What was its name?

I was unable to find an answer. Only when the stars that stayed awake with me had disappeared and the skies became copper-red, I realised that I hadn't slept at all.

In the days that followed, Abba returned to his persona and role as the emperor. He immersed himself in work, becoming busier than usual. The construction of Ammi's memorial was expedited. Abba also ordered the construction of a new fort in Shahjahanabad, to be built with red sandstone. He conducted meetings in Diwan-e-Aam and Diwan-e-Khas. Kushal Khana began to echo again with the sound of musical instruments and dance performances.

I moved into Noor Mahal's Jasmine Palace. It became my home and heaven. This being nearer to the durbar hall, it was more convenient for both of us—for me to join the durbar's meetings, and for him to pay me a visit. Roshanara had been asking for the palace since the time Noor Mahal was banished to Lahore. But it wasn't allocated to her. Naturally, she was angry with me. She read out a letter that Aurangzeb had sent her saying the emperor was partial towards me and her. This upset Abba and he lashed out, saying, 'From now on, there won't be a separate palace for you. You are to stay in Aurangzeb's palace.' When I tried to intervene, he silenced me with a gesture of his hand. Even if we are princesses, aren't we supposed to obey the orders of our father and emperor?

I was hesitant whether to write this. Someone secretly reads what I write. This is the reason for my hesitation. But I am not writing all this for that 'someone', but for my own self. I don't want to hide me from my own self. I cannot lie to myself.

The wounds from the fire were yet to heal. The medicines of the palace hakims didn't work. The scars of memories and the pain from the burns snatched away many nights' sleep. The drink that Hakim ultimately prescribed to induce sleep pushed me into unconsciousness. But I liked it. Nadira was worried that I had become thin due to the potions. Once, I gathered all my strength and stood before the mirror. When I saw my reflection, I screamed in terror. The hijras and maid servants came running and took me back to bed. I knew one of them. Arib Sola, a Parsi girl.

It was either the magic of Arib Sola's fingers or the ointment she brought, but my wounds gradually began to heal. I was able to feel it. I saw scales of my skin falling off, like a snake moulting. Once, when I was in a semi-conscious state, I saw Arib Sola removing my bandages and dressing the wounds with new ones. Someone was helping her. I could guess who it was. But then, I also saw him clearly. Abba. The emperor of Hindustan was attending to his sick daughter. I felt both suspicious and shy. But then, I identified the affection brimming in his Abba eyes and actions. Ya Allah! I let out a sigh of relief.

'Begum Sahiba, not just today, the emperor has been assisting me since the day I started the treatment,' said Arib Sola.

Dulera had stood beyond the fire the last time I saw him. Darkness shrouded my world after that. He went to the battlefield in the Deccan with Aurangzeb. He had sent a *kachli kurti*—as a response to the bracelet I had sent him. It was a beautiful blue dress embroidered with gold zari, and with pearls and diamonds sewn on it. I felt obliged to write a reply, thanking him, and I did write. I appointed an envoy to take the letter to him incognito. He was to stealthily go to Aurangzeb's army camp. And I asked him to bring back Dulera's portrait sketched with hand, or an ivory carved with his image. But the envoy returned empty-handed. Would a battlefield spare anyone time to write letters? Days crawled along in the hope that a reply would come. And it did arrive.

I opened the letter. The handwriting betrayed a hesitation. I realised it wasn't his handwriting. Had he asked someone else to write, perhaps? Doubtful, I read on. Did the Himalayas fall upside down? Did the sun rise in the west? Had iblis taken possession of Dulera? The letter was short and its content clear. 'A Sohan Rajput's image won't fit in a Mughal princess's collection.'

All my happiness died in a moment. Anwari's words in the poem 'Korasan's Tears' came to my mind:

'Originating from a restless soul, the letter ended, slashing something deep inside.'

Why had Dulera written a letter like this? Had anyone informed him that I looked like a burnt log? How could he believe that? I wouldn't have believed even if a thousands yogis had told me something like this about him. Aurangzeb or Roshanara could have told him. Didn't he know that they are enemies to me and Dara? Did the hope that the Sohan Rajput clan was our refuge vanish? I asked myself a hundred questions. Not even one found an answer. I bit my fingers. Thunders hit the darkened clouds. Hundreds of *naqarehs* reverberated. Did a funeral take place in the skies? Or had anything born in the heavens died? Streaks of rains fell. The lightning opened up everything. Then, darkness shrouded it. I was caught within this darkness. The clamour of my broken heart rose from the darkness and scattered everywhere.

The palace lamps were lit after nightfall. My chamber curtains, hemmed with gold and silver lace, were drawn. The entertainment hall echoed with the sounds of musical instruments and applauses.

I rose and stood before the mirror. I looked at my reflection, from head to toe. I was reminded of a story from a Purana, which states that Sita, when she entered the fire to prove her chastity, looked more beautiful than earlier. I also looked more graceful than before. The hair burnt in the fire had now grown back, like a cloud. My face shone like an immaculate moon. My skin being brighter than before, ornaments paled in comparison against it. My breasts were still firm. My waist had grown slender, like an hourglass. And below the waist, the body was full, and the legs were shapely like the hooves of a deer. For a moment, I myself felt enticed by my body. Poor, Dulera! How unfortunate are you!

If everything is God's gift, was my distress also gifted by Him? I will prove that one can live without God.

I paced inside my bed chamber like a cheetah locked in a cage. I could hear an erotic piece being played on the flute and shehnai in the entertainment hall. I rose in fury and changed into the kachli kurti Dulera had gifted me. I put on jewellery, sprinkled champaca attar on my body. Then I went and stood in a corner of the entertainment hall where the drinks were kept. I asked a shocked maid servant to serve me. I marvelled at the way the liquor flowed in an arc from the cask to the golden goblet, as if it were a liquid bow. I gulped down the drink. The half astringent half sweet stream of liquor went down my throat, tickling it.

I stood where the musicians sat. Looking at my shadow, the musicians stopped. They were about to stand up, but I gestured to them to sit. I asked them to stop the erotic music and play something else. They began to play, and the music soared like a waterfall springing from the mountains and gushing into the land. When did I start dancing? Everything around me was swirling. The chain lamps were on the floor and the lanterns were on the ceiling. My soul witnessed my body dancing. I heard the applause. I walked out of the hall like a sleep-walker. When I reached the stone hall near the Feroz Shah stream at the centre of the garden, I heard the sound of the wine goblet breaking.

CHAPTER 4

JAHANARA

A serious debate was on in the durbar. I, Badshah Begum Jahanara, was at the centre of the debate—over the complaints against me and Dulera. *The princess of the Mughal Empire writes letters to the son of an ordinary dancer and sends him gifts. These disgraceful actions will tarnish the name of the whole dynasty.*

I was conducting this durbar. When I recovered from the fire incident, Abba had held a week-long celebration. There were festivities all across the city. Abba donated generously to charity. Gold equal to my weight was given to mosques, madrasas and temples. The title 'Badshah Begum' was conferred upon me. Abba doubled the amount I received as monthly expenses. He allowed me to increase the number of ships I owned in Bengal and Kutch. He also permitted me to levy extra taxes on the Britishers. He also authorised me to conduct the durbar in his absence.

Those who were unhappy with these changes fuelled the debate over my writing to Dulera. I knew very well who they were, but I kept my calm. As the emperor's favourite daughter, I had the right to do anything I wished. No one could utter a word against me. Earlier everyone agreed that like Noor Mahal and Ammi, I too possessed a deep understanding of political affairs. But it had been forgotten now. Should I have trumpetted my own statecraft? If I did, would I be heard by people who turned stone deaf when they chose to? So I kept silent.

It wasn't true that Dulera was the son of a dancer. How could I announce in the assembly that it was my own brother who had spread this misinformation? He had lain in wait for a durbar when the emperor would be away, and instigated others to bring this up. Truly a white serpent! I was burning with rage. The heat of disgrace was fiercer than fire. Concealing my fury somehow, I rushed to my bed chamber, and, tearing my clothes, knelt down like a beggar.

Dulera was a close confidante of the Mughal emperor. He appreciated the fine arts and was gracious. A daring man, he was willing to lay down his life for Abba, Dara and me. That was why Abba had sent him with Aurangzeb. Aurangzeb, however, was good at betrayal. And I fell prey to it.

Dulera was a dancer's son, they said. So what? Didn't Dara Shikoh fall for Ranadil who danced on the streets of Delhi? The emperor got them married without any objection. Didn't Ranadil receive the status of Emperor Akbar's great-granddaughter-in-law and become an equal to Nadira Begum? If a street dancer could become a member of the palace, what forbade Chattar Sal, a Rajput and a ruler, from becoming so? There was a hinderance, of course. While it was a prince who fell in love with Ranadil, Chattar Sal's lover was a princess. Nothing could block a man's path. But there was no place in society for a woman's dream—even if she was Badshah Begum herself.

I stood up and went to the window. Clouds had hidden the stars. I waited, guessing which cloud would move and which star would shine. More clouds gathered and shrouded the skies.

Then one day, Abba summoned Chattar Sal to Shahjahanabad for an emergency meeting. He was to attend the durbar. Panipat brought the news, and my heart was aflutter. But I immediately checked myself. 'Don't get so excited. Like a deer at a mountain stream. This could be a mirage.' I wanted to avoid the evening durbar. But it would be interpreted as me trying to avoid Dulera. Why should I be hesitant, I thought. My mind goaded me: 'If you don't attend the durbar, the rumours will prove to be true.'

Abba used to get easily exhausted in those days. He would fall asleep while on his throne. There was no one to take care of him, except for me. So I always stayed right by him.

I went wearing the kurti Dulera had gifted me. I noticed his face blossom when he saw that. My face stiffened. 'Why should there be a Sohan's portrait in Begum Sahiba's collection?'

When the durbar commenced, Abba made the announcement: he had decided to coronate Dara.

He gave orders to his trusted commanders-in-chief and Asaf Khan to make arrangements for the coronation in the next few days. He asked Chattar Sal to be present in the capital on the day of coronation. Hereafter, he would be Dara's man. After resolving the problems in the Deccan, he was to return with Aurangzeb. Dulera bowed before him and assured Abba of his loyalty. An obedient Dara Shikoh sat in his seat, looking happy. I was happier than him. But I also sensed a fear deep inside me.

While leaving the durbar, I sensed Dulera's eyes following me.

I was thinking about him after returning to the palace. He could come searching for me. I wished he would. The words he had written in his last letter rang in my ears.

'A Sohan's portrait won't fit in a Mughal princess's collection.' It enraged me now. Dulera, you need not come. I will come to you. It's you who are afraid to face me, not I, I thought to myself.

I ordered my maid Koyal to bring me some liquor, and I drank. The liquid fire descended from my tongue like a cold river. On the dark screen of the night, stood a portrait—the portrait with a white silk-turbaned head, a pair of eyes and their thirst staring at me. I drank again to chase the image away. The glasses were emptied again and again. My legs acquired wings and my body fluttered like a peacock feather.

Dulera was staying in the guest house—as a guest of the emperor and emperor-to-be. As my guest too. Wasn't it my duty then to welcome him? I went to his chamber to pay my respects. Did the night fall so soon? But for the lamps, it was dark along the way. A dim night lamp was burning in Dulera's room. I stood silently near the bed he was sleeping on.

The next day, from my balcony, I saw him leave with his regiment.

Was that a dream? Had last night really happened to me? It was all a riddle, haunting my mind.

I was in my bed. Koyal had taken away the goblets I had drunk from. She put out the corridor lamps one by one. She drew the window curtains. The darkness from outside crept in. The fierce cold wind barged in. I was smothered like a rock set ablaze in the freezing darkness. My garments melted and slipped from my body. My ornaments snapped. A moisture spread in my chest. A swirl of nectar descended into my stomach. My anklets jingled. Another body crept up over mine like a cosy burden. Crawling on me, it kissed my fingers, feet, anklets, thighs, and lingered at my hips. Then it descended with a thirst into me as if to introduce itself. My body overflowed with bubbles as if a dry patch of land had been quenched by the rains.

I heard footsteps. They came close and then went quiet. A night bird fluttered and flew away. My feeble mind shrivelled up. It could not bear anything—ecstasy, sorrow or fear. I curled up on the bed. Sleep enfolded me in its wings. A heart-wrenching lament woke me up in the morning. Koyal informed me that the patrol guards had killed someone who had infiltrated the palace last night. So, were they his footsteps I heard last night?

I saw the guards carry away a corpse while crossing Naubat Khana. I asked my maid Hajira to find out whose body it was. 'It's the corpse of the one the guards killed last night. Poor man! He was a singer, they say. They mistook him for a thief. He came to sing before Badshah Begum. He had a costly bracelet on his wrist. Over there, she is his mother. "He never stole anything. He would spend the money he got by singing on charity. Why would he steal?" she says.'

I gave orders to Hajira to write a *farman*. 'That bracelet was my reward for his music. It belongs to his mother.'

An innocent's death plunged me into deep sorrow.

I wanted to lie on the stone bed beside the multicoloured roses in my garden. I wanted to dissolve into the smell of roses. I just wanted to become invisible and touch everything just as the smell would.

Dara Shikoh would become the emperor of the Mughal empire in a few days. Ascending the throne, his first duty would be to revoke the orders of Emperor Akbar. 'Jani, I want to see you and Roshanara get married and live like other women,' he said. He also said that he had found a suitor for me. Who? Nawjat Khan. 'He will be my primary counsellor when I come to power. I am going to talk to Abba about these two things,' he said.

Dara's words comforted and irritated me at the same time. He would set me free from this golden cage. It would be a comfort for Roshanara and Gowra. Not just for me. But the suitor he had found for me?

Nawjat Khan, a descendent of the Palk royal dynasty. An expert at battle and the chess of politics. I had seen him in Diwan-e-Aam on the days the emperor would be away in the harem. But why did Dara choose him for me? Why not Dulera?

Why was I thinking like a fool? No matter whom a Muslim man married, the offspring would be Mughal. If a Mughal woman married a non-Muslim, wouldn't she perpetuate his dynasty? If I married Dulera, *his* line would grow. Wouldn't that be a disgrace for the Mughal dynasty? How had I forgotten this? Who was a woman? Just a machine producing a male's offspring? When I thought about this, I felt nothing but hatred for my dearest brother.

Is it a curse to be born as a female? I felt like wailing. I felt defeated, like the camel in a desert that is unable to carry the weight loaded on its back. The citizens of Delhi should shudder at my cry.

Men have sanctified females simply for their own pleasure. But have they ever known the fire in the veins of women? What is it to a men if a woman, who was created for motherhood, frets, fumes and decays in loneliness? They call it chastity. If a man desires a woman, will her dignity and honour be lost? She sacrifices herself for a moment. She offers up her body. She becomes an object of pleasure. The emblem of sin marked on Hawwa's body still remains.

I was expecting to see Dara. I wanted to meet him before he reached my palace. I wanted to avoid talking to him in my room. Of course, my maid servant and hijras were reliable. But this could change any moment. Such was the state of the palace and the harem.

I went through the secret path adjoining the palace. I wanted to know my destiny as soon as I could. It was not a desire. Desperate, I pushed myself forward to know whether they respected me.

When I neared Diwan-e-Khas, I heard hushed voices. I saw two men there. I hid behind a cactus bush. Nawjat Khan and Jafer, Aurangzeb's close confidants, were speaking as they were descending the stairs. They did not notice me.

'Dara talks as if he has already ascended the throne. As long as I have the strength to wield my sword, he won't ascend the throne. The emperor does not like to approve the idea of getting his daughter married to Nawjat Khan. So is he going to keep her in the harem, as one of his concubines? Jafer, the emperor will have to change his mind. He needs someone valiant to safeguard his throne. Oh! Isn't it the peacock throne? Aurangzeb will fight tooth and nail for it. Just the way the emperor himself battled against Jahangir. That day is not too far.'

As they spoke, they went down a few steps. I cringed. Burning with shame, I tiptoed behind them.

I heard Nawjat Khan's voice again. 'Noor Jahan was witness to the first incident. To this second one, Jahanara. Bhai Jafer, I don't want to become Jahanara's groom. It's Dara Shikoh who is insisting on it. I have seen her. A veil can barely hide her beauty. But we should ask Chattar Sal about the beauty *behind* the veil. Or many others might know too. The walls of Delhi share laughs over this.' Nawjat Khan laughed like a hyena. Jafer seconded with a fox's howl. I stood stunned.

'I know how to safeguard the pride of the Palk dynasty. There is no need for me to marry a Mughal princess for that. Jahanara's veins are polluted with the blood of a kafir. I don't want to disgrace my dynasty by marrying her.'

I had almost reached the brink of unconsciousness. My blood boiled as if my veins would burst open.

'Huzoor, who would dare stop you if you came forward to save Sahibad Al-Samani Jahanara Begum from the enemies?'

'Won't your harem turn into a heaven? If she becomes a part of your harem, won't she be redeemed of her sins?'

'Amir Jafer, if I have to save a lady from my enemy, the enemy should be pure-blooded like me.'

I couldn't hear more. I felt numbed. My tongue went dry. Darkness fell over my eyes. Those two figures vanished. My legs lost their way. I don't know how I entered Mehtab Bagh. Two slaves were digging up soil in the light of a torch. They didn't see me. I didn't want to be seen, either. There were white flowers all over the garden. Their fragrance calmed me down.

Nawjat Khan, don't think you are as majestic as a date palm. You are actually just a chinar, swaying in the wind's direction. You don't have the strength to bear the weight of a woman's sorrow. Other than what you uttered in a fit of anger, what do you know about me?

Will Dulera also think about me the way Nawjat Khan does? This thought made me feel like my heart was being wrenched by iron hands. The cypress trees around me looked like a reflection of my restlessness. Looking at them deepened my sorrow and anxiety. I stood spellbound at the centre of the pain. Choked with fear, I sobbed. The sobs burst out and echoed inside the palace. I saw my maids running towards me. I heard them saying, a snake had bitten Begum Sahiba Jahanara in Mehtab Bagh.

Can a serpent be more venomous than the human tongue?

CHAPTER 5

JAHANARA

No trace of clouds in the sky. It looked like molten silver had been smeared across it in every direction. The sun was a swirling fire. It could burn the eyes looking at it. The sand was brimming with the waves of a mirage. The howling wind threw about the sand. I stood, caught amidst a sand-swirl. The swirls rose and stood as pillars. The pillars closed in on me, and before I could move, I fell into a cage.

My tongue went dry. I was sweating profusely, and my sweat turned into salt crystals. Outside the cage, boys stood holding leather bags filled with water. I waved at them, begging for water. The sand-swirl moved and hid me from their view. I groaned, unable to raise my voice. I open my mouth and begged again for a drop of water. Miracle! Drops of cool water fell on my tongue. My body cooled down, My vision became clear. Drops of nectar fell from the soul. Water flowed from a bowl. I saw the hands holding it. I tried to touch the robe that covered the hands. But it dissolved into clouds. So did my sleep.

It wasn't just a dream but a sign. The room was redolent with the fragrance of kasthuri. A sweetness that I had never tasted before lingered on my tongue. I described at length my dream to Dara's ustad, Mullah Shah Badakhshi, requesting him to interpret the dream.

'Dear daughter, I will tell you about an incident. A Sufi saint asked his disciples to bring some water from the Ajmer pond. The palace guards chased them away when they were drawing water. They returned empty-handed and complained to the saint. He asked another disciple to bring water from Mashkisa. The disciple managed to evade the guards and fill his leather bag. When the bag had been filled, the whole pond went dry. The king and other court dignitaries went to meet the saint. Their pleas melted the saint's heart, and he took some water from his begging bowl and poured it into the dried-up pond. The water spread like a sea and the pond never went dry after that.' Dara and I sat enthralled.

'The hands that had held the bowl and the robe that had hid the hands were Khwajah Moinuddin Chishti's. Now, the dream will make sense to you without my having to explain it.'

Tears flowed from my eyes unchecked. I went to the Anasagar pond. I heard strains of a sweet melody there. The comforting words of the Gracious One, who heeds hundreds of voices, caressed me. They call him Gharib Nawaz. He was charitable to me, who was spiritually poor. 'Ya Khwajah!' I raised my hands towards the skies.

Signs foreshadowed that the days ahead wouldn't be pleasant. Dulera's letter confirmed it. He returned from the Deccan with his Rajput regiment. He came back to Agra, for he could no longer be Aurangzeb's accomplice. He sent me a letter through a messenger to prevent anything unpleasant from happening before he arrived in Agra. Not one but two letters, rolled and kept in a metal box. Apart from these, there was a small slip with the emblem of the kingdom of Bundi. The slip carried these words: 'Badshah Begum, this was the letter I meant to send to you. What you received was a false letter. You know who did this without my having to explain. My original letter was intercepted in the camp itself. But I managed to retrieve it.'

I opened the letter.

It will be the Sohan's honour and good fortune to have his picture included in a Mughal princess's collection.

—Chattar Sal

The emblem of the kingdom of Bundi lay under the signature.

What a betrayal! Aurangzeb, I detest you. My calling you a white serpent is not unjustified, is it? You spew poison on your own sister. Can your five namazes work as an antidote to the poison, Bhai? I won't betray you. But I will add my hatred too when you are hated by everyone else. May Allah forgive you.

I put aside the letter and the slip meant for me and read the other one.

Aurangzeb is gathering an army in the Deccan. He is converting all the minor kings, the rulers of princely states, zamindars and zahidars who were loyal to Emperor Shah Jahan into his supporters. The Amirs, who vowed to give their lives for the emperor are now simply awaiting Aurangzeb's orders.

—Chattar Sal

My heart suddenly felt empty, benumbed. I ordered Naseer to take the letter to the emperor and Dara.

The immediate vision before their eyes simply disintegrated. Other unnerving visions arose in their minds. An overflowing river of blood. Corpses on the bank. Parts of bodies scattered about. Elephants stuck with spears. Horses fallen with legs broken. The grunts of the vultures and the howls of the foxes fighting over corpses. I shuddered.

O death, you come alive before my eyes in human form and look me in the eye with your lifeless eyes. With your cold breath penetrating my forehead, my last hope withers. Oh, sad Hindustan! No blood shed on you could make you whole.

Emperor Shah Jahan's health began to fail. Upon receiving the news, I left for Shahjahanabad that very night. Ya Allah, I was afraid that an earthquake under the feet of the palanquin bearers might shake the very foundations of the Timurid dynasty.

Upon reaching, I recited the Quran, sitting near Abba's bed. I swore on the holy scripture that I would never betray his trust. A braveheart, whom Time itself dreaded; a samrat, who had created such a vast empire, stretching from the Himalayas to the Deccan; a deft sculptor who imagined what no one else could imagine and realised them in stone; the owner of immense wealth, greater than that owned by Badshah Akbar. This man had begun to dread me. How unfortunate!

'Jani, just check, if my hands smell of apples.' He held both his hands towards me.

I was reminded of a fakir we had met a few years ago, who had given Ammi two unripe apples. Abba hadn't forgotten that.

'When the smell of these apples disappears from your hands, know that the twilight of your life has begun.' Abba remembered the fakir's words.

I recalled a question Abba had asked the fakir. 'Will any of my sons rebel against me and seize the empire?'

'Yes. The fairest of them all,' said the fakir. Aurangzeb was the fairest among my brothers. He was ten years old at the time. Abba developed a hostility towards him from that moment on.

All the routes to the palace were closed down. Thirty thousand Rajput soldiers stood guard day and night. The emperor trusted only them. Only Buland Iqbal Dara had the permission to go inside with his friends in the daytime. It was clear that Abba's death wasn't far now.

Dara forbade any news from being circulated. No one could know about the emperor's failing health. But rumours found their way in and out. Rumours were spread that the emperor was dead. Just like the ears of horses perk up on hearing the kettle drum annoucing battle, the enemies unsheathed their swords. Thieves and murderers wanted to make use of this chance. Three days and nights passed in panic. All the shops in the city were closed.

The palace secrets reached their intended destinations through secret paths. Roshanara tactically let the secrets out. Aurangzeb made use of them even more shrewdly. Murad from Gujarat and Shuja from Bengal were bringing regiments to support him. The greed for power which had turned into ashes inside the palace was now burning brightly in the open air. All the sons my mother had delivered, bearing so much pain, chanted the same war cry: '*Ya takht, ya taboot*'.

After a few days, Abba rose from his bed. He wanted to show people that he was still alive. He went to Agra accompanied by his durbar ministers. The news that Murad was coming towards Agra gave the emperor a jolt. Murad was an intrepid warrior, one who had reaped victories in several battlefields. Aurangzeb and Murad joining hands made it easier to defeat Dara. It had been quite easy for Aurangzeb to sow hatred against Dara and reap the benefits. 'Dara is against Islam. The one without any religion. A kafir.' Wasn't this weapon enough to disgrace and defeat Dara?

I desperately wanted to return to my palace. Dulera would have reached the capital. The emperor gave him orders to lead his regiment. But I didn't have the heart to leave Abba. He was so exhausted. It wasn't just disease but his own sons' thirst for power that hastened his senility. In his rose-coloured royal attire, he looked like a hunchback. The king of the world had begun to look like an orphan.

'My dear Abba, how many times did Dara and I plead with you to call Aurangzeb back from the Deccan before he became more powerful than he should be?'

I was a bit harsh. But only after that, the truth dawned on me. Abba came and sat close to me, stroking my hair. 'Dear Jani, who told me that I should forgive Aurangzeb and that I should send him from Gujarat to the Deccan? Who asked me not to believe him? Am I the only one who has been cheated? Didn't he betray you as well? A serpent may look beautiful from a distance. But can one see the cruel poison it hides in its fangs? I had seen the sign of misfortune on Dara's forehead on the sixth day after he was born. On Aurangzeb's forehead, there was a sign of victory. All the seas and oceans and rivers flowing on this earth put together cannot wash off the evil that exists in his wicked heart,' he said.

I kissed his hands. What he said was true. Dara and I had been deceived by Aurangzeb's letters several times. We were never able to decipher the deceit concealed in them.

My mouth went dry. I felt as if Aurangzeb would pounce on me just like a cheetah on seeing the hunter. I buried my face in Abba's weak hands. In a panic, I realised that the smell of apples had vanished from them.

CHAPTER 6

JAHANARA

Dulera gave me a copy of Aurangzeb's letter to Murad Bakhsh.

This is to inform the brave Prince Bakhsh that Prince Dara, known as the heir to the throne, has poisoned our father and taken over the empire. So, Prince Shuja, with a large army, has gone to avenge Dara's betrayal and capture the empire. These circumstances forced me to write this letter to you. Except you, no other prince deserves to be the emperor. Dara belongs to no religion. A non-believer. One who would destroy Islam. Prince Shuja is a religious outcast. He believes in Shia Islam and naturally he is against our community. My reverence for the Quran compels me to consider you the rightful heir. Everyone knows that I renounced worldly pleasures long ago. I want to spend the rest of my life in Holy Mecca. After you come to power with Allah's grace, promise me that you will protect our family members and our father. If you can promise me that, I will use all my powers, skills and strategies to help you. I will do everything I can to see you through to Delhi's throne. Consider this a vow. As a proof of my commitment, I am sending you one lakh rupees. This is a gesture to create a bond of trust between us. We are brothers. Sons of the same father. The Protectors of the Holy Quaran. I end this letter, looking forward to your arrival.

Your brother,

Aurangzeb.

My head lowered in humiliation. I cried, my sorrows gushing out without a pause. Subterfuge! Selfishness! It is a disgrace to the whole family. Will this land, which was ruled by valiant and broad-minded men, turn into nothing? Will this soil be stained with blood forever? Wasn't this land captured by brothers fighting among themselves? Will it always be won or expanded this way? When its original name itself is Kurukshetra, how can this battle for power ever end? Will the air in Delhi always carry the germs that spread the lust for power?

The hot air entered, penetrating the window curtains. My body was shuddering with fear. Dulera stayed silent for a long time. Then he spoke: 'Badshah Begum. We are the emperor's ministers. We transformed our country into an empire. We stood by those who saved it from disintegration. From the period of Chandragupta Maurya and of Harsha, we struggled for it to be united under a single emperor. The great Akbar didn't want to go back, unlike Sultan Babur who went back to Samarkand, or

Humayun, who went back to Bokaro. He wanted to establish his own empire in this land. He wanted to bring the best of other nations here. He trusted and supported us. No one can equal him. If Aurangzeb finds the support he is looking for, this land will no longer be the same. Darkness will devour this land.'

After a pause, enraged, he said, 'Aurangzeb hates us. He wants our support and strength to realise his dreams. But he is afraid of our fearlessness. He doesn't suspect our valour. But he doesn't trust us. He trusts no one but himself. He thinks that the paradise between the first and last pages of the Quran is reserved only for him. Didn't Jahangir and Shah Jahan consider the same scripture the light of their lives? They didn't hate us, did they? We didn't feel insecure during their rule. I have already given my word, Badshah Begum, I will lead the regiment for Emperor Shah Jahan, Begum Jahanara and Prince Dara Shikoh. And I will return victorious. Wait for me, Devi.'

I stood watching Dulera descend the stairs. I desperately wanted to say, 'If I am permitted, I will offer you a sword like Samyukta, or Noor Mahal.' I didn't know why, but I just couldn't say it. Amidst such turmoil, I was thrilled about the moment in which he addressed me as Devi.

The next morning, we saw a big regiment marching forth. Dara's elephant force was with the Rajput cavalry. Chattar Sal's cavalry followed them. Their uniforms shone in the morning light like a river of fire. The Mughal army, the Rajput army and the ministers' regiment.

When I saw the parade and the pace of the soldiers, I thought it would be an easy victory. But destiny awaited Dara with something quite different.

Cannons boomed to hail the march. Trumpets bellowed. Gradually, the sounds and vision of the parade went beyond sight and hearing. For a while only dust was seen. I went to Abba's palace. I listened to his incoherent sentences, reclining on his bed. He was fighting, caught in a maze of confusion. It had become difficult to comprehend him. I turned the leaves of *Baburnama* and started reading aloud, just to grab his attention.

When I read about how Babur's sons Humayun, Kamran, Mirsa Askari and Hindal fought among themselves for power, I was reminded of Aurangzeb. Kamran and Aurangzeb looked like the two faces of the same thirst for power. Kamran too had pretended to be a fakir, and others believed him. When Emperor Babur announced Humayun as his heir, Kamran revolted but didn't succeed. I wished Aurangzeb's revolt would fail as well.

'Times have changed, Jani. This won't end like the previous one. Babur had given orders to gouge out Kamran's eyes. He had said Kamran would destroy the Mughal empire. I can't say that for Aurangzeb. Mirsa Askari kidnapped Emperor Akbar, who was a small child then. Hindal gave his life for Emperor Babur. The Timurid dynasty germinated and its bloodline grew. Allah must have cursed it, perhaps, to be lost, drowned in the same blood ...' Abba said, emerging from his confusion.

What bothered Abba more wasn't Aurangzeb's battle readiness but Dara's reckless courage.

It was the beginning of the month of Ramzan. Bloodshed was forbidden during this holy month. Knowing this very well, Aurangzeb was mustering an army for battle. This made Abba bitter. Dara's son Sulaiman had left to chase away Shuja who was advancing towards Agra in Aurangzeb's support. Shuja backtracked and took him far out. I alerted Dara that it could be a trick. I asked him to wait for Sulaiman's return. His regiment would strengthen Dara's army further. However, Dara's thirst for battle had deafened his ears. He didn't pay heed to my warning.

It wasn't just me. He ignored Dulera's advice too. Ameer Khaleelullah's advice triumphed over Dulera's suggestion to launch the attack on Saturday itself. Aurangzeb's regiment, which had travelled all the way from the Deccan, should have been tired. So, according to Dulera, that would be the right time to attack. This suggestion was undermined by Khaleelullah's reasoning: unfavourable planetary positions. 'The thundering of clouds is inauspicious. Tomorrow is Sunday, the day God created light. Let's wait for one more day.' Dara trusted him blindly. But that day turned out to be auspicious for Aurangzeb. On Saturday, past midnight, the cannons fired thrice. It wasn't the usual fire calling for battle. It was a signal—Aurangzeb's coded message to his men in Dara's regiment. But Khaleelullah told Dara that it was a call for battle. He went ahead and accepted it and gave instructions for the cannons to be fired.

However, Aurangzeb's army didn't march forward. Dara's artillery showered cannon balls throughout the night. It was Aurangzeb's ruse to find out the number of cannons Dara's army had and how far they were. After taking his regiment to a safe distance, for his faithful betrayers to get ready, he blew the cannons thrice as earlier.

'Our artilleries have destroyed most of the enemy regiment. This is the right time. Let's march forward. Victory is ours,' said Khaleelullah.

But Dara's trustworthy commander-in-chief disagreed. 'Let them march forward. We can fight them then. That is safer.'

Dara's mind was riding on his thirst for victory. He stammered, unsure of whose words to follow.

'Prince, the time is right. If you listen to a eunuch like Rustum and delay our attack, we will not see the countenance of the goddess of Victory. We won't even see her back.' These words shook Dara. He rose fiercely and sent the artillery behind and brought the cavalry and infantry to the front. That very moment, his shining star of luck became a meteor, fell off the skies with a cry, and vanished.

Dara's regiment was large in size but untrained for warfare. They had recruited common men who knew nothing about battle. Butchers, barbers, washermen, agricultural workers. It was the first time they were seeing weapons in their lives. They didn't know how to use them. When Aurangzeb's regiment marched forward, they got frightened and fled their regiment. They tried to loot the empty tents and killed each other in the process.

The news from the warfront sent a chill down my spine. What could I do except pray for Dara's contingent? All my time was devoted to prayers.

But Dara didn't care. He egged on his regiment, to march forward and attack with courage. When the army scattered, Aurangzeb's cannons began to boom. Dara's soldiers were unsettled. They were surprised by the enemies' joint forces. Chattar Sal and Rustum Khan hastened towards them for help. They penetrated Aurangzeb's musketry and scattered their camels and infantry. They missed their aim and shot their own men. Aurangzeb hadn't anticipated this. He acted instantly and sent more forces to the battlefield.

The warfront reverberated with hostility. Swords clashed and shone. Trumpets bellowed. The trumpets of the elephants, the grunts of the camels, the neighing of the horses and the howls of the foxes were heard together. Bows shot arrows fiercely. The quivers were frequently refilled with arrows. Prince Dara was egging the soldiers on from his howdah. It did have an impact, for the enemies were stabbed, shot at and stamped upon.

CHAPTER 7

JAHANARA

A restless Agra woke up tensed and terrified. The spies reported that people on the streets were anxious about the war. The common people who lead normal lives were unable to understand the reasons behind such battles. They weren't quite aware that the quarrels within the palace impacted their lives as well. They didn't understand why they had to be slaughtered in a battle between unknown people. I imagined myself as one of them. Why do I become a prey to my brothers' battle for power? Why are women held hostage for the sake of men's greed for power? Questions riddled me and plunged me into despair. I felt like a broken-winged bird imprisoned in a golden cage.

A British soldier on a horse galloped towards the palace. When he reached the palace's courtyard, his horse collapsed on the ground and died. He said that Dara's arsenal had been destroyed and the government's regiment was losing. How could I believe him? After a while, an envoy from the battlefield arrived, announcing Buland Iqbal's victory. How could I believe this either? At that juncture, both victory and defeat seemed meaningless and futile. I didn't want to believe anything.

Abba's life defeated him in a matter of days. I had no words to comfort him. I would blankly stare throughout the day from my balcony.

The sun was scorching the earth. Dust spread like a shadow of bad omen and shrouded the stars. One couldn't see anything, only listen in the darkness. I was able to listen to the sections of cavalry marching towards the palace. But there was no sign of anyone entering the palace. Why had no one come in? In the first half of the night, the noise of the horses' hooves transformed the wind into a cyclone, nearing us with each passing hour. Gradually, the noise faded away. Did the hurt horses move away? Why didn't the soldiers have torches in their hands? I inferred that the horses were being taken towards the stable.

Dara returned. But he didn't go past the courtyard. He must have been afraid that the enemies would imprison him. Perhaps he didn't want me or Abba to see him in his pathetic state. But he sent an envoy before going to his palace. I was with Abba when the envoy came. He paid his respects and repeated Dara's message: 'Emperor Shah Jahan's predictions have come true.'

Abba insisted that he be sent to the warfront. It wasn't to wield his sword against the enemies but to thwart Aurangzeb's lie: the emperor lies powerless and weak.

The emperor's presence would motivate the soldiers. Dara turned down the proposal. I sent one of Abba's trustworthy hijras to comfort Dara.

This was what the hijra said upon his return:

'Aurangzeb's scattered regiment had dispersed. A time came when he himself was about to get caught. He had sent the soldiers on horseback to stop and chase away Dara's regiment. Sitting atop his elephant he declared that he wasn't afraid of battle and victory was his only aim. Had Dara chased the soldiers a little further away, he could have presented Aurangzeb and Murad in shackles before the emperor. But at that very moment, the prince announced rest.'

The soldier in front of us—grimy with dust and drenched in blood—looked like the herald of defeat itself. He seemed to have come to prepare us for what we didn't dare to hear earlier. But I was now mentally prepared to listen to anything.

He continued: 'The soldiers attacked when Dara was at rest, and Amir Rustum Khan was martyred. While fighting with Nawjat Khan, King Chattar Sal was shot dead. I was cursed to witness all this. Perhaps, this is the result of my sins.'

He broke down. What he said didn't even reach my ears. His mouth, hands and body spoke like a dumb puppet. I also stood like an immobile puppet. Had Khaleelullah Khan come to the rescue after these two casualties, the battle wouldn't have ended this way.'

What the soldier said wasn't true. I rose to say that it couldn't be true. But I fell back in my chair as soon as I rose. I didn't want to listen to anything else. I went to the balcony, leaving Abba alone. As if a pair of cruel hands with sharp talons closed in on my heart, I felt suffocated.

I sat as if under a spell in front of a door that opened to the river Yamuna. Koyal came and stood near me. 'Begum Sahiba,' she stammered. When I turned back, I saw her eyes were moist. She said between tears that a soldier from King Chattar Sal's cavalry had brought a message which was meant only for me.

My heart jumped with ecstasy like a spring in the desert. I ordered all the lamps to be lit and all the curtains to be pulled open. I felt the touch of a cool breeze after a long time. He, who came limping on his injured legs, fell on his knees and bowed at the centre of the hall. There were wounds all over his body. Blood was oozing from them. I asked Koyal to bring medicines and applied them to his wounds. He was an untouchable. But I treated him like one of my close relatives. Being Dulera's soldier, how could he be an outsider to me? He began to speak, with much difficulty. But how can I repeat everything he said? I will write all of it on these anxious papers with trembliing hands.

'When thousands of Dara soldiers were retreating, Chattar Sal crushed Nawjat Khan's cavalry and gave Murad a chase. He was fierce enough to imprison death itself. "Cursed are the lives of fugitives. We are bound by the principles of the Kshatriyas. Our dharma is battle," he exhorted others. His elephant, struck by the fire ball of a cannon, staggered, threw him down and ran away. "My elephant may accept defeat, but never his master," King Chattar Sal declared and mounted a horse. At that very moment, a bullet from Murad's gun pierced his forehead.'

I sat in silence. I was careful not to miss a single word. I was praying that the soldier's blood flow wouldn't stop and his pulse rate wouldn't fall. If he died, who else would tell me about the last moments of my beloved? The light of his eyes was intact. Was it the last light of life?

Still on his knees, the soldier took out a pearl string from under his turban and held it before me. Pearls washed in blood!

'Hit by the butt of a gun, I fell unconscious. When I came to, the enemies had left. There were just corpses all around. Amidst them, the lifeless body of my king Chattar Sal lay abandoned. Only after I identified his dead body, did they take him to the tent. No one noticed this pearl string that fell off his hands when they lifted his corpse. I thought, or rather my king's soul made me think, that it should be handed over to the princess, as a keepsake from my king, who was a trusted ally of Emperor Shah Jahan.'

I held out both my hands to receive that holy reward. Removing my veil, I wore the pearl string, and it came alive between by breasts.

'Badshah Begum, I am the only witness to this truth. It wasn't Murad's bullet that defeated my king. It was Nawjat Khan's hostile bullet. I was too far away to alert my king to it. It was my misfortune.'

Falling on the floor, he broke into tears as if begging for forgiveness. I was looking at him with frozen eyes.

'Badshah Begum, what took place there was not a battle, it was a fight for power. A competition between the one who deserves it and the ones who think they deserve it. People like me, who are completely irrelevant to this, are losing our lives. Forgive me for uttering these words in front of you. Badshah Begum, this would be the last time the Rajputs marched under the flag of a Mughal emperor.'

He rose and slowly moved towards the door to take leave, dragging his broken legs. There were bloodstains in the spots he stepped upon. The marks of grave misfortune.

CHAPTER 8

JAHANARA

Leaning on a pillar in a corridor of the palace, I sit facing the Yamuna—as if it is the very source of my life. Hands with sharp talons still gnaw at my heart. But I am able to breathe without any difficulty. My blood boils with pain, hatred and the desire for revenge. I just can't bear this turmoil any longer.

From a rowing boat in the river, a song floats over. A male voice. Amir Khusrau's song. They come from several centuries ago—the voice and the verses. I have heard the lyric innumerable times. They run in my veins.

> *Penury is better than pomp*
> *Fall is better than devotion*
> *Flamboyance is a headache*
> *Eventually, begging is better*
> *If sorrows break your heart, better give in*
> *and break down than remain a slave*

The lines seep into my heart, and moisten my eyes. It is better to be a *fakira* than a Badshah Begum. It is better to roam like a beggar than be a slave in a palace. But that is not within my powers. I have none. No one wants me. I am the shadow of loneliness. No, I am loneliness.

I realised something, as if by magic. My body has suddenly become weightless. I have been liberated from the body made of skin and blood. My body turns into air, water and fire at will. The Yamuna flows under my feet. I feel myself dissolving into her currents. I hear the flowing river. My voice is also heard like the murmur of the Yamuna. Both, my voice and the Yamuna, turn into music. Their duet sounds like a music concert I listened to in Delhi, where a rendition by someone made several people shed tears. The Yamuna carries me away, far away from the banks of life. It cleanses the insults and injuries I have suffered in my time on earth. Everything becomes clear to my inner eyes. I am not in this world at all. I have come a long way from there. I adorn myself in garlands of champak flowers. Holding them, I stand amidst the princesses of the heaven.

I want to narrate my story to myself. The story is over, but my grief isn't. I write as if I were wound up. I write everything. Sometimes, I write after long breaks. I am telling this story to someone other than me. To whom? To forgetting, which is powerful. One day, it will turn into memory.

The night after the battle of Samugarh, Koyal found me asleep on the floor, with my arms embracing the pillar. Without the heart to wake me up, she put a blanket on me. Past midnight, I experienced a strange transformation. This gave me strength to bear any misfortune.

Murad was quick to trust anything. He trusted Aurangzeb's words, which Aurangzeb uttered swearing on the Quran. 'I am a fakir. I am not interested in power. You deserve to rule this empire, not Dara. This battle is being fought to win the throne for you.' Murad trusted these words and allowed Aurangzeb to lead his regiment. My foolish brother, even a simpleton understood that Aurangzeb knew when to wear a fakir's tatters and when to don the robes of power. How did you forget this?

One cannot blame Murad. Aurangzeb planned everything perfectly. He got help from Shaista Khan who hated the emperor. When? At which moment did Amir Shaista Khan, who was greatly trusted by Abba, turn into Aurangzeb's shadow? It wasn't just Shaista Khan, but many others who were loyal to Abba shifted allegiance to Aurangzeb. No. Aurangzeb lured them into this with false promises, or threatened them to yield before his powers. He sent letters to governors and royal representatives to help him find Dara, who had fled the battlefield. They weren't simple letters, they were warnings.

Aurangzeb sent a similar letter to Emperor Shah Jahan too. 'I am your son. My aim is to save you from Dara Shikoh's clutches. The battle was just for that.'

Abba sent a reply in the same tone. 'The battle was a trick to trap Aurangzeb. Isn't he a white serpent?'

We were wondering how to escape this ordeal. Aurangzeb's sugar-sweet words had taken away most of our trustworthy Amirs and commanders-in-chief from us. How could the common folk come to our help without a leader to lead them? We spent our days and nights thinking about this. Abba wrote to Aurangzeb, asking him to come and meet him in person. Aurangzeb was clever. From the letter, he decoded Abba's plans. He knew about the female fighters of the Tartar tribe that the emperor had appointed as his bodyguards. He knew that if he came alone, those women would pulverise him, and he didn't reveal his fear. But he sent a message every day that he would pay a visit but never turned up. At the time, he was getting ready for something else.

One day, Aurangzeb camped with his full regiment at Taj Mahal. A crowd of traitors had gathered under Amin Khan's leadership to welcome him.

Abba called for the only trustworthy commander-in-chief left with us and made him sweep the fort for security risk. He asked all the entrances to be closed. He asked for the cannons to be prepared, but it was too late. Aurangzeb's regiment had already besieged the fort. They took over Dara's palace. The soldiers came past the port walls. We were imprisoned. No one was permitted into or outside the palace. The granary was closed down. The ovens of the bawarchi khana were extinguished. Food and drinking water were denied to us. The servants, patrol soldiers, the ladies in the zenana and the hijras who had held their peace for a few days, started cursing us.

'Jani, I can't take it anymore. The worst of all curses is hurled by a stomach burning with hunger. Should I bear this too? Tell that serpent that I concede, and we will hand over the keys to the fort. Ask him to come to the durbar.'

Abba fell on his knees and lamented. The ruler of the Earth implored like an orphaned beggar.

I still remember the servants who carried away the keys. The jangling of the keys still echoes in my ears.

The day Aurangzeb came after evading the invitation for weeks turned out to be the first day of our decline.

Aurangzeb entered with a huge army, but didn't go to the durbar. He went to Abba's palace and stood at the entrance. He signalled to me to come out. I was near Abba. When I refused, I saw his face grow stiff and red. The fire in his eyes pushed me forward. When I reached the entrance, I heard a laughter. It was Roshanara's laughter. She stood glittering in garish garments and jewels. Her poisoned teeth shone with contempt as she laughed. The pride of victory sparked in her eyes. My legs were rooted to the spot. Darkness clouded my eyes. I could hear Aurangzeb's voice from far away.

'I seek your forgiveness, Abba. From this moment on, I assume the responsibility of ruling the Mughal empire. I claim your throne. No, you don't have to rise from your bed. Not just now. You can just stay in bed hereafter. That is safer for you. If you think this is a prison, then this is the most suitable place for you. Don't try to blame me. I have learnt these tricks and rules from you. We are responsible—I, for thanking you, and you, for applauding me. I have done to you just what you had done to your father.'

'You, white serpent! Get out of my sight!' Abba screamed, his eyes fraught with hatred.

Aurangzeb turned towards me. He looked dreadful, like a hooded serpent. He looked at me with a venomous wrath, and then left without a word. He left like a snake emitting poison. His army followed after.

The next day, he sent a letter to me and Roshanara. He asked us to leave Abba's prison and to stay in the harem. I sent a reply that I would rather spend my whole life in a prison than lead a luxurious life with traitors who lust after power. 'You fool! You spoil your own life,' Roshanara mocked me. She sent back Nazir, who had brought the letter, and went to her chamber. Then, she came out all decked up and doused in perfume. She went past me and stood at the entrance to Abba's room. She looked at our old father lying shrunken in bed, and smiled mockingly. That was the last time they saw each other.

CHAPTER 9

JAHANARA

Everything I write here is based on the information gathered by my spy. I would rather trust his words than my own eyes. When I heard what he said, I was devastated. I was awake, praying as the night faded into dawn.

Murad Bakhsh and his army set out in search of Dara. He went halfway back to Agra on Aurangzeb's orders. Then he rested in Mathura. The battle was just like a leisurely tour for him. Everyone knew that Aurangzeb wouldn't crown him. Murad himself heard about it from others, but his hopes remained up for two reasons. One, Aurangzeb had sworn on the Quaran; and two, the confidence in his own warfare skills. Murad's army's victories in the Gujarat region had bolstered his confidence. But he had learnt no lesson from them. On the contrary, he was inebriated with pride. And in the army camp arranged by Aurangzeb, Murad spent most of the nights drinking and making merry.

He believed that the discussions that went on in Aurangzeb's tent were for his coronation ceremony. New caparisons for each elephant. New saddles for the horses. New tents were pitched on the river bank. Men and women gathered. New clothes were brought on golden platters and jewels arrived in silver boxes. Many kinds of delicacies were cooked in the kitchen tents. Songsters and dancers performed day and night.

But Murad was drinking away in his luxurious tent. Khwaja Shabas, who was like Murad's own shadow, warned that Aurangzeb had different plans. But Murad never heeded the warning, and Shabas's words of caution were lost to the wind. Murad refused to listen to his trusted advisor Ibrahim Khan too.

Would anything that threatened or surprised human beings become their destiny? Aurangzeb had become our destiny. He was just like a lurking cheetah, awaiting his prey. He didn't hunt for hunger but for fun. For power. To show his powers to the world. Murad was too immersed in wine and daydreaming to notice that he was the first of Aurangzeb's preys.

Aurangzeb's retinue welcomed Murad to the tent prepared for the coronation. Aurangzeb took him to his chair. Music and dancing were on. The fragrance of flowers, the sandal smoke from the frankincense burner and the smell of tobacco from the hookahs floated in the air. Aurangzeb's confidants and those who were believed to be Murad's confidants were permitted inside the tent. Murad didn't even register the naked mockery of this act—he was simply being welcomed as a clown.

The feast commenced. Various kinds of food and wine were served. The guests' goblets were refilled before they emptied. After a while, Aurangzeb told Murad, 'Bhai, go get some rest. I will call you at the time of coronation.'

Murad returned to his tent with Shabas. A beautiful woman stood waiting for him there. Shabas sent her away. 'Huzoor, a trap is being laid for us.' But the hijra's words couldn't jolt Murad back to his senses.

'Before the prince could realise that Khwaja Shabas's fears were not unfounded, everything was over, Begum Sahiba,' so saying, my spy paused. I cannot write what he said after that pause. The pause was meant for him to gain the courage to narrate the rest of what had happened. It's not my hand that writes what he recounted, but the hand of an iblis called destiny.

Murad lay on his bed, inebriated. Shabas sat on the floor, massaging his legs. He didn't see Aurangzeb coming in. He stood up when all of a sudden he saw Aurangzeb, who stood inside the tent, wearing his white robes, without a cap on his head, scratching his beard. He signalled to him to go out. Shabas made to leave, when four guards gagged him at the entrance and whisked him away.

When Murad woke up, he found himself in shackles. The weapons he searched for in fury had been removed. Nothing could be done. He shed tears. Wearied, he looked down, hanging his head in shame. He murmured silently, 'Aurangzeb, is this the promise you made, swearing on the holy Quran?' On Aurangzeb's orders, soldiers closed in on Murad.

Two elephants left the riverbank that night. One for Agra and the other for Delhi. Murad was tied to the back of the elephant headed towards Delhi. When the elephant moved, the soldiers in and outside the tents screamed on top of their lungs: 'Mirza Muhi-ud-Din Muhammad Aurangzeb Alangir Bahadur Ghazi!' Murad saw his own 'confidants' amidst them.

Though Aurangzeb dressed like a fakir, it was Chengiz Khan's blood that flowed in his veins. Each time he advanced fiercely in the race for power, the verses of the Quran dissolved in blood.

Insulted and injured, Murad was reduced to a street show. Slaves holding swords surrounded the elephant. Their swords were ready to behead him if he tried to escape. A small cell whad been prepared to imprison him, if he stayed alive. Murad submitted himself to destiny.

'Begum Sahiba, I cannot bring myself to describe what I witnessed after this. Spying over the evil, I am afraid that my own body is poisoned now ... Poisoned sherbat was given to Prince Murad in the prison. And the innocent hijra Khwaja Shabas's body was hacked into four pieces.'

He fell on his knees and prayed. Abba's voice was heard from a corner of his bed chamber—as if it was the voice of darkness itself. 'Ya Allah, not one of my sons has stood by me in the twilight of my life. I don't have the shade of their loyalty.'

Long after the spy had left, his words still echoed throughout the hall. Abba and I couldn't sleep that night. It was a night without an end.

I bury my face in the sheets as I write about my brother Dara. Let my tears touch the ink. My tears aren't colourless. They are black with despair.

Dara fled the battlefield and reached Lahore. With the help of the trust and respect he earned there, he was able to muster an army again to fight against Aurangzeb. The minor kings who didn't like Aurangzeb also pledged support to him. None of my brothers could win the hearts of others like Dara. His bright eyes and sweet voice helped him garner support. But Aurangzeb's warning reached the farthest corners of the empire and the neighbouring countries beyond it in the form of a letter, threatening Dara's allies. Many who had promised support went into hiding.

Dara was shocked. But he was determined not to concede. Submission was out of the question. Death was certain, if he got caught. But he wanted to walk into the jaws of death fighting against Aurangzeb. Placing his trust in the Creator, he gathered an army again, and began his march towards Gujarat.

My pen is too worn out to write about the incidents that shook the empire that had been built and extended under Emperor Shah Jahan's sceptre. Abba believed that his empire would outlive him. But that wasn't what his sons thought. They fought against each other, chanting, '*Ya takht, ya taboot!*' either the throne or the tomb. Poor Shuja didn't even get his tomb. He lost against Aurangzeb and fled to the riverbed of Airavati. Wild animals feasted on his corpse. Shuja was the first to challenge Abba's rule and disrupt peace. How sweet he used to be … how energetic … but the greed of power distorted him into someone else.

Jaswant Singh, the king of Gujarat, who fought alongside Emperor Shah Jahan in many of his battles, agreed to send his army with Dara. Dara's hopes were revived. He prepared to march towards Agra.

However, on the day of departure, Jaswant Singh called his army back. His own life and throne were dearer to him than his loyalty to Abba. Who could escape the clutches of Aurangzeb? And so, Dara's second attempt at battle also ended in failure. He lost all his supporters.

The last nail in the coffin: his trusted commander-in-chief killed his own soldiers, instead of wielding his sword for Dara. The rest of the army ran away.

If one's destiny has been woven with black thread, can it be turned into white, even if washed in the water of Zamzam and Kausar?

CHAPTER 10

JAHANARA

The final darkness was inching closer to my brother Dara. Gujarat, which he had always considered his home, shut its doors tight. Burdened with failure, Dara had sought refuge in a land shrouded with heat and dust, but it chased him away. The shut doors thus crippled all his hopes. The sobs from the women's tents and restless prayers seeking God's grace added to the heat of the sun and made the nights darker than usual. I was pondering over why God makes human beings, weighs them down with misfortune on earth, and then calls them back at will.

Prince Dara was abandoned by all his old friends. After the second defeat, a big part of the regiment left him. He stood like an earth-forsaken man, without anyone by his side. Aurangzeb's regiment kept continually chasing him away, without giving him a moment of rest. Dara drifted from one place to the next with his retinue that comprised his wives, Nadira Begum, Udhipuri Begum and Ranadil, his daughter Jani Begum, his son Sabir

Shikoh, and a few thousand soldiers who were still loyal to him. How far could he go with so many people? Exhausted, Dara headed towards the north to try his luck. Persia was his destination. His retinue travelled for miles without stopping anywhere. But fate awaited him at his final destination, to pull him into the black void of its lap.

His destination was the city of June on the borders of Persia. Malik Jivan, the ruler of the Persia was in Dara's debt. Dara had saved his life once. Malik Jivan would have found his grave at the hands of Emperor Shah Jahan's wrath had it not been for Dara's help. But now Malik's heart wasn't filled with gratitude but with terror. He sent a message about Dara's arrival to Aurangzeb. He imprisoned Dara's family and the soldiers who opposed him. The city of June became Dara's final destination. Not just for him, but also for his family and those who loved him.

Nadira was the light of our palace. She was the perfect one—Ammi's choice. She, who flew like a pigeon, was now trapped in a prison. She shuddered in horror and fretted in despair. She knew that she couldn't live without Dara. She understood what her fate would be without him. She would be forced to become one of the concubines of Emperor Aurangzeb. She seethed with fury and burst into tears. 'This is my gift to the avaricious devil waiting to feast on my husband and sons' blood!' In an unexpected moment between her sobs, she swallowed the diamond set in her ring. A moment when Time offered Dara a cup of poison. My dearest brother swallowed it, his hands shuddering.

The prison house reverberated with cries and lamentation, and outside, the clangour of weapons and the exultation of soldiers were heard. Aurangzeb's soldiers besieged the city of June. 'Handcuff the prisoners,' they shouted. Their shouts leapt over the walls of the city. Before Dara could unsheath his sword to fight the enemies and be martyred before the eyes of his wives and children, he was put in handcuffs and shackles. There were four elephants with howdahs waiting to take him and the others back to Delhi.

Dara and his family were locked in cages, and these were mounted on the elephants. Dara's two wives were put in one howdah, his son and daughter on the second one, and Dara's cage was loaded onto the third elephant's howdah. To guard the cages on the howdahs, there were henchmen with swords. No one knew in which of the four cages Dara was kept. The number of soldiers increased as the army moved out of Persia and onwards. When they reached Delhi after forty days, the army looked like a giant battlefield on the move.

They took Dara—on the elephant, caged and in handcuffs—through the streets of Delhi. The subjects who said salam to Buland Iqbal Dara looked at him and tears welled up in their eyes. A fakir from the crowd howled amidst tears, 'Huzoor, you gave me alms when you were the master, but now you have lost everything ...' Dara threw his soiled shawl towards the fakir. Before it could fall down, a soldier on horseback caught it midair, wound it and threw it away. A prisoner had no right to give alms or gifts.

After the enquiry, Aurangzeb wrote the verdict. Dara had championed idolatry. He was an enemy of Islam. He would be beheaded for these crimes.

There isn't just one path to God; there are so many ways of reaching Him—as many as there are human souls. Dara searched for his God in different ways. Would his painful death have shown that there were rules etched in stone, which mortals could not trespass? Would it have proved that no language could reveal the ties between the creator and the created? Dara, my brother, may Allah's grace be with you till the day this earth exists.

On the next day, news arrived that Aurangzeb had sent Abba and me a gift. What could the white serpent give us? What else could he gift other than venom? On seeing the gift he had sent on a copper platter, Abba screamed. I was too stunned to even let out a cry.

The gift on the platter was our dearest Dara's head—with blood oozing from it.

CHAPTER I I

JAHANARA

Aurangzeb crowned himself for a second time. The first was to bring the soldiers and commanders-in-chief to his side. The second was to announce his authority to the world. A warning to his opponents to hold their peace.

Left with no alternative, Dara's slaves, concubines and hijras sought refuge in Aurangzeb's harem. Dara's second wife, Udaipuri Begum, yielded to his orders and agreed to be tied in the cattle-shed of his lust.

'What else can I do, Begum Sahiba? I am just an orphan, one of the numerous slaves bought in Georgia. I see no other way to save my life. I don't want to kill myself like Nadira Begum. I was known as one of Dara's wives, but after his lust for me died down, he counted me as just one among the miscellaneous crowd in the zenana. I was merely a slave who didn't have to beg for food and clothing. My body was simply a grassland to graze on when the prince found other women's bodies lacklustre. Now, Alamgir Aurangzeb has occupied the grazing land. There's no difference. It's just the same. There is a verse in our Bible, which says, human beings are born of dust and to dust they shall return. I don't want to go back as mere dust, Begum Sahiba. I don't want to die as an orphaned beggar.'

In all these years, Udaipuri Begum had rarely ever spoken to me. I even doubted whether she could speak. This was the first time she opened her heart. I hugged her, but she released herself from my embrace and vanished into the harem forever.

Obeying Aurangzeb's orders, Udaipuri Begum saved her life. Ranadil defeated him, sacrificing her life. When Naseer went as an envoy, asking her to come to Aurangzeb's harem, she sent her back with a question: why should she come? The emperor wanted to marry her—came the reply. 'What makes him want to marry me?' she hissed. Then she cut off her thick hair and sent it to Aurangzeb. 'Didn't he like my hair? Take this to him.' The fool didn't get it. Aurangzeb sent for her again. It was her ravishing beauty. He wanted to marry her just for that. The envoy returned. 'You need not accept him as Aurangzeb, it's enough if you take him as Prince Dara.' Ranadil's fury knew no end. 'I was a lowborn, dancing on the streets to make a living. Dara Shikoh sanctified my femininity with his love. He made me honourable. I will never accord his place to someone else.' These words must have deepened Aurangzeb's obsession. He sent her letter after letter after letter. She threw them in the fire without reading them. Then he sent some hijras to convince her. Ranadil's fierce eyes chased them away. Finally, he sent hijra Koja Phul who knew well his personal affairs. Koja was an expert in the tricks of defeating women. But nothing worked with Ranadil. Koja's tricks began with 'Alamgir Aurangzeb cannot forget your beautiful face' and ended with the alluring words, 'He will make you the Queen of queens because your beauty just makes him lose his mind.' Ranadil slashed her face with a dagger, and, wiping the blood off her wounds with a kerchief, gave it to Koja. 'Your Alamgir likes my beauty, is it? Isn't it for this that he troubles me? Here it is. Take this to him. Let him be happy with this.'

Koyal looked as if she had woken up from a nightmare, when she described this. 'It's good that you didn't see Ranadil like that,' she said. I wouldn't have, even if I had to. A face as impeccable as the moon seen on a pool's surface. How could I see her as a bloodied moon?

I requested the durbar hakim to treat her. He was hesitant at first. He was afraid of Aurangzeb's reaction. I forgot that under Aurangzeb's rule I had no right to command anyone. When Aurangzeb permitted the hakim to tend to Ranadil, I understood that I still had some powers. But Ranadil refused to be treated. Her wounds worsened and pus oozed from them. Her skin decayed and fell off. Her hair too. She lost her teeth. She refused food and medication.

'Begum Sahiba, she may listen to you, perhaps,' said Koyal.

At first, I didn't want to. I didn't want to see Dara's dream sculpture reduced to a heap of stones. I had seen the most mutilated human beings until my eyes smarted. The mind is afraid to see lifeless bodies—bodies without heads, heads cut off from the bodies, chopped off limbs. But Koyal insisted. 'Is Ranadil a lifeless body? Isn't she a soul? Isn't the body an ornament? It is not right to ignore the body.' A voice kept echoing inside me. I went to see Ranadil. But she didn't give me a chance.

I saw from the balcony—her corpse being carried away by the hijras in a coffin with no decoration. All she got was an orphan's funeral. What else can a prisoner like me do except pity her? Ranadil was also a prisoner. But she was able to defeat Aurangzeb. She was able to insult his authority, mock his lust and cripple his pride.

I saw someone at my door, a reluctant figure trying to peep inside from behind the curtains. It was Jani—Jahanzeb Banu Begum—the name my dearest brother Dara had given his daughter to show his love for me and Ammi.

I ran and took the child in my arms. I felt as if I were hugging my own childhood. Her young, slender body was trembling. I sat her on my bed. When I hugged her tightly, her sobs melted into tears. 'Ammi Jani,' she cried out.

'What happened?'

Only tears flowed in reply to my question.

It was just then that I noticed Koyal at the door. She gave the answer.

'It was I who brought her, Begum Sahiba. She was crying alone in the garden. I took her to the harem. But

Begum Roshanara threw her out. I couldn't bear it and brought her here.'

Jani had Nadira's face, Dara's eyes. But she was thinner than the children we had seen in the famine-stricken Deccan. There were scars of wounds on her hands and legs. Dust shrouded her skin. Was she the same child whom Nadira always carried in her arms saying her feet would get dirty if she walked on the ground? I felt a fierce fire ranging inside me.

I handed Jani over to Koyal and asked her to bathe and feed her, and then I ran towards Abba's bed. His welled-up eyes conveyed that he was a witness to all that was happening.

The Quran states that it is a sin to punish the innocent. Aurangzeb, who followed the scriptures, conveniently forgot these verses. He arrested all the male heirs of his elder brothers—the potential threats to his authority. He imprisoned them in the Gwalior fort. He murdered a few of them with poisoned sherbat. He could have killed this child too, instead of handing her over to Roshanara, like throwing pearls at swine.

'Jani, look there!' For the first time in months, Abba's voice was clear and spirited. Trying to turn on his side and sit up, he said again, 'Look over there!' His shivering right hand pointed at the inner door. My gaze followed his hand. Jahanzeb Banu Begum stood there like an angel descended from the heavens. Abba and I said in unison, 'Alhamdulillah!'

CHAPTER 12

JAHANARA

The hot summer air assailed Agra. But I felt cold as if I was in Kashmir. It was a sign that someone close to my heart was about to come. But who would come to this palace-prison?

My loved ones had plunged me into the darkness of a solitary life. My dearest Ammi, my beloved Dulera and my brother Dara Shikoh—everyone had forsaken me. Abba, who loved me the most, was crippled, spending his days simply staring at the wonder of wonders he had built for Ammi out of marble. He would listen keenly for the footsteps of death. He screamed in fear, waking up from nightmares. He lamented his own wrong deeds. Emperor Shah Jahan, who once made his enemies tremble in fear, was now afraid of his own self. Putting his head in my lap, I caressed him to allay his fears. He sheds tears thinking he had punished me.

'Calm down, Abba. With Allah's grace you will have many more years to live. You will see little Jani grow up, you will experience the contentment of raising a daughter, something you didn't get the chance to do with me.'

I knew they were just empty words, with no meaning. Whenever I said those words, I would hide my tears from Jani.

My intuition wasn't wrong. Mullah Shah Badakhshi arrived like a breeze in a furnace. He first went to see Abba who lay in bed. But Abba didn't register his presence, for his eyes were fixed beyond his window, on the Taj Mahal. Mullah's greetings couldn't break through his reverie. He came away.

'Forgive us, Ustad. Abba's mind isn't really here nowadays. His eyes see nothing but the Taj Mahal.'

He smiled softly and said, 'Love is the light of the world. But now it is hidden like the sun behind the clouds of Hindustan. Clouds are not permanent. They will certainly go away. The Gracious and Merciful One will drive them away.'

Mullah Shah Badakhshi took his leave, but his words kept ringing in my ears for several days afterwards. The moist mercy in his words and their power unfolded into visions.

I saw a huge forest in front of me. The hilltops were visible. On the slopes stood cedar trees, like the guards of heaven. The entire forest bloomed with flowers of various colours. Not a drop of human blood was shed there. Walking through the saffron garden and the rose beds, I stepped into the shade of the trees that had sprouted new leaves and reached a hilltop. The mountains had kept a secret for me. A formless voice began to reveal it, a voice I had never heard before. The comforting voice of the Creator. But before the voice could reach my ears, I heard a cry.

'Begum Sahiba, look at the emperor,' Koyal's weak lamentation tugged at me.

Abba was on his knees, facing the west. Both his hands were stretched out towards the skies. His lips were moving. For the first time in eight years of imprisonment, his voice was so clear and without stammer. Abba was reciting the kalima. I went down on my knees before him.

'La ilaha ill Allah, Muhammad-ur-Rasoolullah ...'

After he recited, he lay down on his bed, as if he had let go of a huge burden. After a few moments, he rose and looked in the direction of the Taj Mahal. He kept looking at it. The eyes of my Abba, who was known as Abul Muzaffar Shaha-ud-Din Mohammad Shah Jahan, were wide open even in his death.

Everyone gathered in Abba's room. Dara's daughter Jani, Abba's wives, Akbarabadi Begum and Fatehpuri Begum, his concubines, slave hijras and Koyal. Aurangzeb was sent for, but he chose not to come. 'This son won't forgive the father who didn't forgive him' was his reply to the messenger. Had my anger had the power to burn, it would have burnt him to ashes. But isn't anger just a flickering flame within a glass lamp?

The news of Emperor Shah Jahan's death spread along with the darkness of the night. A huge crowd gathered around the fort, but the gates were locked down. Only two from the people thronging outside were allowed inside: Mir Sayyid Mohammad Qanauji and Agra Khaji.

No king of the Timurid dynasty had been given such a funeral. A braveheart who had conquered lands in all four directions, a statesman who had expanded the Mughal empire, filling its coffers with immense wealth, a visionary who had built grand cities, a lover who loved with unparalleled loyalty and affection, the emperor who had dreamt of a greater Hindustan—a man such as him was covered with a shroud made of coarse cotton cloth. His body was laid in a coffin with no embellishments. There was not even a jasmine petal on the coffin of this man who had been a great gardener himself, who had nurtured separate gardens dedicated to each flower. This king who travelled all his life on the royal path atop elephants or in chariots was simply allowed to leave through the back gates for his final journey.

'At this late hour?' I turned furious. The light of the Mughal empire was to be taken like an orphan in the dark of night. The subjects were denied their right to see their beloved emperor and say goodbye. Seething with rage, I protested. But Koja Phul, Aurangzeb's faithful slave, didn't heed my words at all.

'Alamgir Aurangzeb's orders are to conduct the funeral before dawn. And it is my duty to obey his orders,' came the reply of the heartless devil.

I was so exhausted. My body felt scorched, as if I had been pushed into a pit of fire. My vision blurred, as if a darkness shrouded my eyes. I cried, 'Abba', but my voice was muted. The sound of Agra fort's back gates opening ripped through my heart. I ran and peered through the jharokha. Carried by four bearers, Abba's coffin disappeared into the black void of the night. As it disappeared, I became aware of a light gradually seeping into my soul. I felt as if I was being freed from something. I had been now released from all shackles.

It wasn't dawn yet. Laments in hushed tones resonated through the palace. The cries that burst out loud faded into whimpers. I slowly walked towards the balcony. The breeze blowing over the Yamuna was turning cold. In the silence of the night, the river's flow was crystal clear. I could hear the birds flatturing in the dark. I looked up at the sky. It was endless and dim, and without a trace of a cloud. But the faint shine of the crescent moon was still visible to the eye.

AFTERWORD

'My hands quiver as I write. I keep my thoughts secret. How else can I survive? Am I not a woman? On this lonely night, I sing my despair into forgetting. Tonight, I narrate my story into forgetting. My story and my despair.'

—Jahanara

This is not a historical novel, albeit history serves as its background and historical figures appear in its plot. It is coincidental. While writing it, my intentions were different. One can take refuge in history, for one can't always openly express the present. If the past can manifest itself in today's history, I presume we can find traces of the present in history too. Can't one witness family politics and inheritance of power—which is debated at present—in the past too? The genesis of this fiction lies in this question.

I tried to handle history, which serves as the backdrop to this novel, 'factually'. I believe I have succeeded to some extent. The details I have used here are true. The incidents described are true. Most of the characters mentioned are true. Research papers provide evidence for that. Wherever the incidents were very sparsely described, I fleshed them out with facts gleaned from historical documents. I found these additional facts in the same data. While attempting this fiction I realised there are several untold episodes in history, and thus, history can never be considered the absolute truth, holistic or impartial.

There is a common notion that there is a chapter in history, which ignites interest, seen from every possible angle: the Mughal period. I found this to be true while writing this novel. The chance encounter that led to this realisation has a name: Jahanara. This name and the search for it were unexpected.

I happened to spend a few days towards the end of 1993 and the beginning of 1994 in Delhi. I went there to take part in a translation workshop conducted by the Sahitya Akademi. It wasn't unusual for me to visit the historical spots and monuments of Delhi in the evenings—at times alone and sometimes with acquaintances and friends from the Delhi literary circle, including some Hindi writers. One evening I visited the Hazrat Nizamuddin Dargah with my friends. We walked around the premises, which housed many tombs. I saw the tombs of several lesser known Mughals, poets and Sufi saints. A few tombs had crowds gathered around them, performing rituals of remembrance. There were people who offered prayers and those who complained, burying their faces in the walls. Two tombs stood alone, with no offerings being made to them. They caught my attention, the tombs of Amir Khusrau and Jahanara Begum. I knew Khusrau was a poet and I often listened to his heart-melting ghazals. And so, his tomb held significance for me. A few steps away from Khusrau's tomb was an open mausoleum with marble pillars. Without a roof, this tomb was exposed to the skies. This seemed unusual, for Mughal tombs were almost always housed inside enclosures. The tomb I saw in front of me looked like a box left open. This difference piqued my curiosity. The sentences inscribed in a calligraphic style on the tall headstone looked enigmatic. When I asked my friend Anjan Sen about the tomb, I came to know that this was Princess Jahanara's tomb. She, who had lived and died three hundred years ago, entered my heart that Friday evening and etched herself into my subsciousness like an everlasting shadow.

I read widely on Mughal history, but in phases. During one such phase, I was drawn to Sufi literature and music. This phase revived Jahanara in my memory again. When the Imam from Nizamuddin Dargah had spoken about those who followed Sufism, I remember he mentioned Jahanara's name too. Her tomb should be open to the skies, there shouldn't be any decorations except the grass that grows naturally around it—this was her wish, which is inscribed on her tomb's headstone. The Imam explained that this was in adherence with Sufi thought. Jahanara identified herself as a disciple of Khwajah Moinuddin Chishti, who foregrounded the Sufi tradition now predominant in India. She wanted to free herself from the royal luxuries and battles for power and follow the Sufi tradition. However, women were not encouraged to follow Chishti's tradition. So, Jahanara's wish never came true.

My wish was to simply write a poem about her. When I attempted it, it dawned on me that Jahanara could never be contained within a single poem.

An arduous search took me to two books, which helped me get to know her: Kathryn Lasky's *Jahanara: Princess of Princesses* and Andrea Butenschon's *The Life of a Mogul Princess: Jahanara Begum*. These two were the grounds from which the seeds of this novel sprouted. Both these books have been written in the form of a diary. While reading them, I realised that Jahanara's story would fit well in this form.

All the Mughal kings who ruled India recorded their lives in diary entries. Their everyday life and achievements were recorded in diaries. Beginning with Babur, the first emperor of the Timurid dynasty, till Aurangzeb, everyone kept a proper record of their lives. A few of them wrote their autobiographies too. Those who could not write like Babur appointed others to write for them. These accounts came to be known as *Baburnama, Akbarnama, Ain-e-Akbari, Humayun-nama*. Noorjahan—Shah Jahan's stepmother—religiously made notes on the everyday durbar proceedings during Jahangir's period. But Jahanara is the first Mughal woman to have maintained diary. Her entries were more personal in their tone too.

Kathryn Lasky narrates the events in Jahanara's life between age thirteen and seventeen. Jahanara hadn't begun writing at this age. So Lasky's written her novel in the form of imagined diary entries. I see this as Lasky's attempt to add credibility to her fiction. There are both historical and fictional characters in this novel. I see it as fiction based on Jahanara's life. On the contrary, I see Andrea Butenschon's book as being closer to the non-fiction available on Mughal history.

Andrea Butenschon belonged to a family that migrated from Germany to Sweden. She was interested in writing since she was young. She was the student of Ellen Fries, a teacher, feminist and the first woman to receive a doctorate in Sweden. When Andrea came to India between 1890 and 1891, she visited places like Bombay, Delhi, Agra, Jaipur, Varanasi and Calcutta. A strange incident in the Agra Fort shone light on Jahanara after two hundred years. Andrea happened to enter an abandoned chamber in the Jasmine Palace, where Jahanara had lived. She put her hand on a wall to lean against it, and the wall crumbled. The stones dropped to the floor, and from behind where the wall had stood, fell out bundles of paper, wrapped in leather. There were writings on those papers, in Persian. It was discovered that they were the diary entries of Jahanara Begum. Later on, translated by Andrea, they were published in book from in 1932.

Aurangzeb imprisoned Shah Jahan in 1658. The imprisonment lasted for eight years, till Shah Jahan's death. For the love of her father, Jahanara also spent those eight years with him in the prison. What Andrea found in the fort were her diaries written during the imprisonment. The pages give clear insights into Jahanara's personal life, the political turmoil, battles and assassinations that took place in her time at the hands of Aurangzeb. She had hidden her diaries, fearing the unpleasant consequences if they ever happened to be discovered.

She had written: 'I hide these papers under the stones of the Jasmine Palace. Someday, the palace will become dilapidated. People will find my autobiography under its debris.'

She was the eldest of Mumtaz Mahal's five children. Jahanara was considered wise and astute enough to discuss and advise on the durbar's affairs by her father, the emperor, when she was barely fourteen. There was a separate throne for her in Shah Jahan's durbar. She was highly influential, and wealthier than any other in the royal family. She was out of ordinary. She knew more than three languages; she read poetry. She read epics; she had read the Vedas and the Puranas, all the religious scriptures. She learnt music and dance. She was well-versed in architecture. She owned ships. She lived in a separate palace, and she had her own coffers overflowing with wealth. She had everything, yet she was allowed something that she thought would have made everything else lesser in comparison. She was a woman who had been denied the right to marry. Won't this tragic deprivation be sufficient to write a novel on Jahanara?

I stayed in Sangam House, Hessarghatta, in 2013 and wrote a large part of my first novel, *Wellington*, there. I got an opportunity to stay there again for a month. It was there that the idea of writing a novel about Jahanara based on her diary entries struck me. I completed the first part of the novel in a month, and a full year rolled by riding on that contentment. Another writers' residency came to my help and bridged the gap in the writing. I got an opportunity to stay at the Toji Cultural Foundation, Wonju, South Korea, in September 2017. The Toji Cultural Foundation is an independent space for writers and artists created by Pak Kyongni, one of the pioneers of modern Korean literature. Surrounded by mountain ranges and dotted with farmlands and dense pine forests, it is a serene place two hours away from Seoul. I completed the novel in this serene place. The Toji Foundation library and YONSEI University library helped me clear my doubts.

The Mughal period is a segment of history that is much explored by historians. There are umpteen books on Mughal rule. There would be hundreds of books dedicated to individual Mughal rulers, from Babur to Aurangzeb. And there are books on the Mughal women too. Jahanara, however, hadn't been written about much. She had merely been described or quoted as a witness to the tussle between Shah Jahan and Aurangzeb. Compared to the research done by historians on her grandmother Noorjahan and her mother Mumtaz Mahal, the research material available on Jahanara was very sparse. Perhaps this bias against, or let's say, history's ignorance towards her drew me to her. I took an oath not to read any fictionalised narrative on Jahanara before completing my novel. Jahanara herself stood by me as an invisible muse, helped me stay on course.

I used only the diary entries written by her. I arrived at a framework, picking entries as they were and narrate them in my own language, adding alongside some fictional scenes whenever she fell silent. And so, this novel unfolds in Jahanara's words, and the moments unknown to her, or the events she could not have witnessed or voiced, were written through other characters.

After completing my novel, I read the other novels based on Jahanara's life. And I let out a sigh of relief: my Jahanara was different from them. There were several novels, written in English as well as translated into English from Hindi and Urdu, which had been received well. Indu Sundaresan had published a very successful trilogy set in the Mughal era: *The Twentieth Wife* (2002), *Feast of Roses* (2003) and *Shadow Princess* (2010). The last book told Jahanara's story. Ruchir Gupta's *The Mistress of the Throne* (2014) was also based on her life.

I read these novels to seek clarification on just two important aspects. The first one involved Jahanara's love life. Akbar had passed a law barring Mughal princesses from marriage. So, Jahanara and her sister Roshanara lived as spinsters. But many historical documents mention that Jahanara had suitors. I wanted to see how these existing novels had handled this. Indu Sundaresan portrayed Nawjat Khan, one of the trusted commanders-in-chief of Shah Jahan, as her lover. I found that frame unsuitable because in her diaries Jahanara refers to him with contempt, as 'a sycamore tree swaying to the wind's direction.' Ruchir Gupta portrayed Gabrial Bowden, a British doctor, as her lover. Jahanara met with a fire accident on her thirtieth birthday. There were references to this English doctor, who came and treated her on Shah Jahan's invitation, and in return, receive lands in the Bengal territory for the East India Company. However, I thought this could not be the reason for Jahanara to fall in love with him. Jahanara has given a detailed account of the fire accident in her diary. She mentions no one but the Parsi slave who treated her and brought her back to life. So I decided to avoid portraying these men as her lovers, although I did mention that Nawjat Khan was considered by Dara Shikoh as a suitable match for Jahanara.

The second confusion that I wanted to clear rose from the notes of Niccoalo Manucci's travelogue. Manucci was an Italian traveller and writer who visited Shah Jahan's durbar. He came as a tourist and stayed on in India. His writings give a detailed account of India under Mughal rule. He was a frequent visitor to Shah Jahan's palace. As his notes are believed by historians to be credible, it led to a confusion. He wrote that there was an illicit relationship between Jahanara and Shah Jahan. However, Francois Bernier, a French traveller who visited India during the same period discredits Manucci's accounts. He says it was just rumour spread against Shah Jahan and Jahanara. So in my novel I cautiously created an air of enigma with regard to their relationship.

Many supported the evolution of this novel, at various stages. Arshia Sattar, D.W. Gibson and Rahul Soni, who were in charge of the Sangam House Writers' Residency; Radhi Jaffer and Aparna Rajesh at the Indo-Korean Centre who helped me with my stay at the Toji Cultural Centre; Kong Pok Yung from the Seoul Arts Centre and Yeo Jee In, the director of Toji Cultural Centre—all of them provided great support during the initial stages. Their hospitality helped move my writing forward. Kannan Sundaram of Kalachuvadu, the originator of all these avenues, has stood by me throughout.

Gharib Nawaz Moinuddin Chishti's dargah in Ajmer was the origin of Jahanara's spiritual quest. She donated a large part of her income to this dargah. It is believed her donations have been preserved there to this day. I wished to visit the dargah, and my wife Prema made the wish come true. She read the manuscript, highlighting its shortcomings. My friend Navin made me feel like a modern-day badshah during my trip to Ajmer. Taj Jagadeesan, one of my friends from Abu Dhabi, was my first reader, and he gave me useful feedback on the manuscript. K.N. Senthil guided me out of my dilemma about the climax. T. Rajan shared his views on the novel's structure. G. Kuppusami, Reena, Shalini, A.S. Padmavathi and Yuvan Chandrasekar read the manuscript too and shared their views.

Without Kalandhai Pir Mohamad's support, the novel wouldn't have attained its current form. He helped clear my doubts regarding Islamic terms and rituals. Jeba proofread the novel. Kala Murugan formatted it. My friends at the Kalachuvadu office, Senthuran, Eswaranadhan, Valliyur V. Perumal, Shuba, Manju and Manikandan, were also of great help in various ways. Rohini Mani recreated Jahanara for the cover of the original Tamil edition, making her way more beautiful than I had imagined her to be while writing the novel.

My heartfelt thanks to every one of them.

Now, the English translation is in your hands, and I sincerely hope you will enjoy reading it.

Sukumaran

www.ingramcontent.com/pod-product-compliance
Lightning Source LLC
LaVergne TN
LVHW011009200726
843509LV00011B/1033